CASTLE OF ST. REM

TOWER OF GRATZ

CASTLE OF BEAUCAIRE

THE GYPSY CARAVAN

"... But the dwarf replied: Only the
light of heart may travel here, for this
road leads to enchantment!"

—OLD TALE

BOOKS BY
HOWARD PEASE

THE TATTOOED MAN

THE JINX SHIP

SHANGHAI PASSAGE

THE GYPSY CARAVAN

"What wonderful adventures we've had!" Betty exclaimed

THE GYPSY CARAVAN

Being the merry tale of the travels of BETTY *and* JOE
with the GYPSIES—*their amazing adventures with*
ROBIN HOOD—*with* RICHARD *the* LION-
HEARTED—*with* ROLAND—*and sundry*
other great and famous persons.

BY HOWARD PEASE

ILLUSTRATED BY
HARRIE WOOD

YOUNG MODERNS

DOUBLEDAY & COMPANY, INC.

GARDEN CITY, N. Y.   1950

TO

"BOOTS"

SOMETIMES KNOWN AS
DAVID EUGENE CARY

CONTENTS

CONTENTS

ILLUSTRATIONS

"*The most beautiful adventures are not those we go to seek.*"—STEVENSON

I

The Taxi Man

"HOLD tight!" called the Taxi Man. "It's happened!"

With a shrill grinding of brakes the car came to a sudden halt. The boy and girl who had been sitting sedately on the cushioned seat slid to the floor in a most undignified manner.

"What's wrong?" gasped Betty.

"Maybe we hit something," her brother answered as he rose and peered from the window.

The Taxi Man jumped to the ground and opened the door. "It's happened," he said serenely. "I knew it would."

"What?" asked Betty.

"Oh, I've blown out a tire," he explained. "I'm very sorry, but you'll have to wait till I fix it." He threw back his cap and gazed uncertainly at his fares.

"Wait!" cried Betty. "Oh, but we can't. We're going to a party—a masquerade party—and we're late already."

The Taxi Man shrugged. "Sorry, but I haven't an extra tire with me and I don't think there's a garage on this country road. It won't take long—perhaps half an hour or so."

"Half an hour!" wailed Betty. "We're late already. That's why we came in a taxi—and now it's broken down!" She lost her frown and, as she saw the look on the Taxi Man's face, her own mouth wreathed in a dimpled smile. She straightened the rose-colored handkerchief tied gypsy fashion about her head and ran her fingers through her golden-brown curls which escaped from the confining folds. "Well, I suppose we'll have to wait," she continued.

Joe jumped to the ground. "We might walk," he said. "It's not far from here—just down the road, I think."

The Taxi Man smiled. "It might not be a bad idea to walk," he observed to Joe. "You like walking, I can see—because you're just the sort of chap that little dogs like. And you're both dressed as gypsies. What kind of a party is it?"

"It's a masquerade party," Betty again explained. "Everyone we know is going. It was so far and we were so late that Mother ordered a taxi for us. I'm eleven and Joe's nine years old, you know, and this is our first ride in a taxi. And now it's broken down!" She was near to tears.

"We'd better walk," broke in the practical

Joe. "Anyway, who ever heard of gypsies riding in a taxi!"

Betty, pausing on the step, gazed sadly down at her dainty green slippers. "My new slippers will get all dusty!" she said with a fretful shake of her curls. She straightened her gypsy frock and smoothed its ruffles of red and green. "And as for riding—if Robin Hood can ride there, I should think that gypsies could."

"Robin Hood!" echoed the Taxi Man. "Is he going to be there?"

Joe nodded. "Jimmie's going as Robin Hood— and there'll be a Charlemagne, too—all in armor."

"And Roland," Betty continued. "And Richard the Lion-Hearted."

"Whew!" gasped the Taxi Man. "This is a regular storybook party."

"It's Helen Wright's idea," said Betty, as she stepped to the ground. "We're to call her house a Castle of the Middle Ages. We're gypsies come a-begging. They call us Dark People of the Dark Ages. It's going to be lots of fun."

Joe grinned. "We really ought to have donkeys to ride on. Or a gypsy caravan—a house on wheels." He glanced about as if he hoped to see several donkeys grazing by the roadside and a gypsy campfire blazing near by.

"Shall I call for you?" asked the Taxi Man.

Joe shook his head. "No, Helen said she'd bring us home."

The Taxi Man waved them down the road. "Good-bye," he called. "Give my regards to Robin Hood!" He chuckled as he turned to repair the tire.

Joe led the way. "We must hurry, Betty," he urged. "We don't want to be late."

"Are you sure you know the road, Joe?" Betty asked. "Look, there are four roads here."

"This is Four Corners," Joe announced. "I think our road is the one that turns to the right."

"There's a sign over there, Joe. What does it say?"

Together they crossed to a yellow sign which had an arrow pointing to the right. It read:

H O M E
Three Miles

"Well, that's not our road," said Betty.

They looked about. They stood at a crossroad where four country lanes wound away over gently sloping hills.

"It must be the road to the left," remarked Joe. "Let's start that way."

Betty, somewhat doubtful, followed him. It

was early afternoon and the sun was warm and cheerful, yet Betty glanced anxiously about. On both sides the trees rustled mysteriously; the lupin and goldenrod growing by the roadside nodded their heads and whispered; and the vagrant leaves went spinning merrily after them.

A steep hill faced them, and up this they quietly trudged. "We ought to see the house from the top," Joe remarked.

Betty nodded. On they went. At the crest they paused, tired and dusty. Before them the road dipped and rose to a second hill. Betty turned to Joe, but his brown eyes evaded her glance. "Where can the house be?" she asked.

"It ought to be here!" he replied. "It ought to be——"

Betty looked at him in scorn. "If you ask me what I think, Joe—I think we're lost!" She dashed a tear from her cheek. "Yes—I think we're lost!"

II

The Strange Road

"OH, NO, we're not lost," said Joe manfully. "It's over the next hill. We'll go that far, anyway."

Betty agreed, and on they went. Once a rabbit leaped across the path and disappeared into a thicket. That was the only living thing they saw.

"Everything is so strange—and still," Betty murmured.

She drew nearer to Joe as the road plunged into a dense wood. A wall of beech and fir rose on each side. Even their footsteps were silenced by the carpet of leaves. The air was cool and fragrant with the scent of growing things: wild berries and mint, ferns and damp pungent moss. Somewhere in the forest depths a bird suddenly caroled a little magic song.

Betty slackened her pace. "It's getting dark, Joe."

"A fog's coming up."

"A fog?"

9

"Yes—coming in from the sea."

It was true; a soft haze that had hovered over the tree tops now seemed to descend, to deepen into dark blue and purple and entwine itself about the firs and beeches.

"Let's hurry," Joe urged. "I'm sure just ahead——"

On they hurried through the wood. The thickening fog clung to them with caressing dampness. The trees grew indistinct and ghostly. The road seemed to dwindle to a mere path, ever winding up and up. Hand in hand they trailed on through the misty gloom.

"Look!" Joe whispered. "The fog's lifting."

The country seemed to be vaguely swimming about them. Far ahead the rays of the sun touched the edge of the fog bank; it glinted on a thousand points of light. Betty and Joe stared. The sense of having left the real world behind possessed them. They had strayed into a dream country; about them lay enchantment.

From a near-by hedge a bird twittered. Betty whirled. "I believe someone's following us," she whispered.

"You're imagining things," Joe answered, without a backward glance.

Betty stood on tiptoe. "Something is coming along the road behind us," she continued.

Abruptly she clapped her hands. "It looks like a band of gypsies." Both joy and fear were in her voice.

"Gypsies!" Joe exclaimed. He turned in sudden disbelief.

III

The Gypsies O!

YES, gypsies were coming. Down the hill and along the road crawled the red and green wagons of a caravan. Breathlessly Betty and Joe watched as the procession approached.

With a tinkle of bells the caravan came toward them. First appeared a lone horse whose small heels pattered gayly on the roadway; next came three ponies, who stopped now and then to crop the tender grass by the wayside. After them followed the wagons.

What gay vans! One was green like a meadow in spring, and one was blue like the sea. Both had little white windows with still whiter curtains blowing in the breeze. The third van was scarlet with bright gold trimmings, and the fourth had a round roof with two small gables on each side. Several more wagons followed— homes on wheels, all painted gaudily and all the abodes of dark-skinned gypsies.

As the first wagon drew near, Joe stepped to

the side of the road. It was the green van and was driven by a very old man.

"Where are you going?" Joe called.

The gypsy pulled up his ponies. Taking off his hat, he revealed a pair of soft dark eyes and long gray hair that almost reached his shoulders. "Anywhere," he replied; "anywhere the road leads."

Joe and Betty glanced at each other in surprise. Surely this was a strange answer. Anywhere! Who ever heard of going just anywhere!

Joe touched Betty's arm. "Wouldn't it be fun to ride."

"Oh—we wouldn't dare!"

The gypsy regarded them intently. "Where are you going?" he asked.

"We're lost," Betty announced.

The old man pointed to her gayly colored frock. "A gypsy lost!" he exclaimed. "Never have I heard the like before. But we be Romanys, too. You can have a lift—and welcome to it. Jump up."

Joe helped Betty to the seat of the green van; then he jumped to the other side of the driver. The gypsy flicked the reins and the ponies started along the winding road.

"This is better than walking," Betty remarked. "I'm even too tired to talk."

The old man looked down at her and smiled. Betty stared, for the gypsy reminded her of the Taxi Man. Over gently swelling hills they went, where sheep grazed amid the wild flowers. Meadowlarks sang from the hedges, and now and then a startled rabbit bounded away into a thicket.

The gypsy, smiling, turned his bronzed, wrinkled face to Joe. " 'Tis well to have company on the road these days," he remarked. "You never know whom you may meet."

Joe was watching the two ponies with great interest as they went mincing along. He was thinking what fun it must be to lead such a gypsy caravan as this, going anywhere—everywhere—just for the sheer joy of going. At the gypsy's words he looked up.

"But you are never alone on the road, are you?"

"Sometimes," the old man replied in his low, steady drawl. "When the business of the road is bad—when tinkering and lace selling and fortune telling are not what they should be—the wagons separate. We always appoint a day and a town in which to meet. On this road we travel together."

He turned to Betty at his right. "Be careful, little one, that you don't fall beneath the wheels."

"Oh, I won't fall," Betty answered. "I'm only looking back at the other wagons. There are seven, Joe—and each painted a different color. Aren't they pretty?"

"We were talking business," said Joe, "about tinkering and selling."

The gypsy smiled. "And about the people one meets on the Great Highway. Robbers and vagabonds are as plentiful as berries along the road's edge."

Betty looked up quickly. "Robbers!" she whispered.

"Vagabonds!" cried Joe.

The gypsy nodded sagely. "Oh, we Romanys meet everyone. Around each turn lies adventure. . . . Who knows what may be waiting for us around the next bend of the road!"

In Which We Encounter
Robin Hood and His
Merry Band

SECOND MILE

"*Tidings came to bold Robin Hood*
Under the greenwood tree;
'*Come prepare you then, my merry men.*
We'll go yon sport to see!'"

BALLAD

I

Sherwood Forest

ADVENTURES!" said Joe. "Oh, we're always looking for adventures—aren't we, Betty?"

Betty glanced round at the unknown, beautiful country through which they were riding. "Yes," she agreed, turning to the gypsy; "but Joe always has one kind. He gets into trouble."

The old man chuckled. "Well, then we'll have to look out for Joe, because this road to Sherwood Forest is a dangerous one; outlaws, thieves, soldiers of the King, all abound here. And, of course, the gayest rogue of the lot—Robin Hood."

Joe looked in amazement at the driver. "Did you say Robin Hood?"

"Robin Hood, of course. Everyone about here knows that famous scamp. Ah, he's a merry chap; he plays pranks sometimes on the well-fed folks, but he is kind to the poor peasantry. Only to the miserly rich is he a hard foe."

"And he really lives here?" Betty breathed.

"In Sherwood Forest yonder. You can see the great greenwood trees from the next hill. There he dwells with his men—an open, carefree life he leads, akin to us Romanys in many ways. Often has the King's agent, the Sheriff of Nottingham, tried in vain to capture this Robin Hood; for he's like a mouse who may nibble the cheese, yet runs not into the trap. Ah, he is a man—Robin Hood—and dearly beloved by the country folk."

Breathless, Betty and Joe listened while the gypsy told many an exploit of the bold outlaw. On down the hill wound the caravan, through a shadowy dale where a tiny stream blocked the way, and up again over the next rise. Here they could look across to the vast forest which drew ever nearer on their right hand.

When they had arrived at the top of one of these hills, there came through the trees before them the sound of a voice singing a lilting ballad of old romance. The gypsy urged forward the ponies; his face was alight with expectation.

"Who is it?" asked the inquisitive Betty.

"Sounds like Alan-a-Dale," returned the old man. "He is ever sitting on a stone wall singing of the beauty of the day."

Betty stood up on the seat to look ahead. "Do you mean that it's Robin Hood's friend, the troubadour?" she eagerly whispered. "Oh, I've heard of him! He sings wonderfully, I know."

They came to a shaded spot where a cool spring gurgled from the bank and went in a merry little stream down the hillside. Seated above the pool upon a lower limb of a great oak was a gayly dressed youth who blithely strummed a lute and sang as though he were serenading the trees about him. At sight of the first wagon of the caravan he brought his song to an end and, hopping from his perch, came toward them with outstretched hand.

"By holy St. Dunstan!" he cordially cried, "it's Stanko the Gypsy back once more to Sherwood."

"Were the Romanys ever known to miss a fair at Nottingham?" the other rejoined. "Ah, 'twas a jolly song you were warbling as we came up, Alan-a-Dale! But why are you not with the outlaw band?"

"Hush!"

Alan-a-Dale looked warily round, then spoke in a whisper: "Travelers on the King's Highway are not yet all friends to Robin Hood and his merry men. One must not speak the name too loudly lest enemy ears pick it up and babble to the agents of the King. Listen, it is a secret. Robin Hood has gone to Nottingham!"

The gypsy's eyes widened. "What! He has even dared to go into the camp of his enemy, the Sheriff of Nottingham? Why, 'tis madness! Every archer in the shire wants the reward offered by the King and will be looking for him."

Alan-a-Dale threw back his head and laughed. "Yes, but the King's men will be searching for a bowman in Lincoln Green, and Robin is disguised. No man will know him; he is too clever for that." He picked up his discarded lute; strumming it for a moment, he hummed a gay tune.

"But why did my good friend Robin endanger himself by entering the town?" asked the gypsy. "What takes him there?"

The singer stopped and again looked about him. "Do you not know that to-day there is a prize contest? The Sheriff has proclaimed a shooting match; the winner will get a cunningly wrought arrow of gold. It is the Sheriff's idea that Robin Hood will not allow anyone to surpass him

in archery, that he will come to the match and so
be taken prisoner."

Betty and Joe clung breathlessly to every
word.

"And so Robin goes like a lamb into the den
of the lion!" mused the gypsy. "Oh, Robin,
Robin, what a bold rogue you are!"

"Tell no one," warned the singer.

"Stanko the Gypsy does not blab like a
thoughtless girl.   Perhaps I shall see this Robin
at the Fair. How is he dressed?"

Alan-a-Dale shook his head in perplexity.
"None of the band knows. Robin thought this
such a dangerous mission that he desired no
chance remark to get out—as if one of us would
tell of his whereabouts! Why, 'tis unthinkable."

"Of course," mused the gypsy, "only an im-
practical poet and singer would let his tongue
run away with itself. But let no one know of this,
for I surmise that exciting events lie ahead."

He flicked the reins. "We tarry too long. On,
Mimo! On, Zulieka! We must hurry to Nottingham Fair."

II

Nottingham Fair

LONG before they reached the town they saw far off through the trees the gleam of the tan and red tents at the great Nottingham Fair.

"Look, there are flags, too!" cried Betty, pointing out the slender banners of blue and red floating against the golden sky. "Oh, it's a wonderful fair—a wonderful fair!"

The gypsies made camp on a gently sloping hill above the town. Nottingham lay in a cool valley, a town of old stone houses and narrow winding streets. Outside the walls, in a meadow immediately below the gypsy camp, were pitched the tents of the Fair, all crowded at this hour by the townsmen and the peasants from the neighboring countryside. The shouts and clamor of the multitude floated up to the camp like the hum about a summer hive.

After Betty and Joe had helped Stanko tether the ponies in a grassy glade they built a camp fire near his green van. Other gypsies, staking

out their tents or grilling a partridge over an open fire, paused to look with curiosity at the two strangers. To their questioning glances, however, Stanko threw a reassuring reply in an unfamiliar tongue.

"Romany talk," he explained. "Our people

like not strangers within the camp. *Gorgios* they call you—foreigners; but you are welcome to stay this one evening with us. More than that I dare not promise."

Joe looked up quickly. "Can't we stay with you any longer, Stanko?"

"I fear not. 'Tis a rule of Romany life that each member of the tribe must bring in his share of money at the fairs."

Betty sighed. "Can't we work—can't we sell silks and laces?"

"We all hawk our wares through the town. Can you make things? Can you weave baskets or do fine needlework—or tell fortunes?"

Betty and Joe sadly shook their heads.

"You haven't learned much, have you?" went on Stanko. He stroked his chin thoughtfully, then his bronzed face broke into a smile. "I would that you two might travel with me in my green van. 'Tis lonely there, even though I be chief of the tribe."

"Chief!" cried Joe. "Why, then, of course, we can stay if you'll let us."

The old man slowly shook his head. "Little ones, try to understand. Even a chief cannot change a law of the tribe. . . . Come, let us eat."

The odor of frying bacon mingled with the acrid smell of wood smoke. Joe sniffed hungrily as he renewed the fire. Betty sat on the little steps that led to the ground from the back door of the van. A stir among the gypsies, which presently rose to a loud wail, caused her to look inquiringly at her friend.

"Meg the Fortune Teller hasn't arrived yet," he explained. "We left her cart at the Blue Boar Tavern in Banbury to have the axle mended. At fairs we make most of our money by telling fortunes, and now Meg, the Chosen One of the tribe, has not come."

"Perhaps she lost her way," Betty suggested.

The old man shook his head. "We left *patterans* at each turn of the road as we came; she'd never miss them."

"*Patterans?*" Joe asked.

"Our signs by the roadside, known only to the Romany folk—little pieces of wood placed in positions which point the way to us but which are passed unnoticed by the *gorgio*."

Betty suddenly uttered a little cry: "Joe, you're burning the bacon!" She seized a wooden fork and went to the rescue. "Of course, I couldn't expect you to cook a real meal," she continued with the corners of her mouth twitching. "No man can."

Joe moodily poked the fire. "I was thinking," he explained.

"Thinking!"

"Yes—if only you could tell fortunes!"

In surprise Betty let the wooden fork drop to the ground, where the handle began to smolder in the blaze. "Tell fortunes?" she repeated. "Oh, I couldn't—I don't know how."

Stanko suddenly turned from the fire. "The very thing," he agreed with a chuckle. "You must learn to be a fortune teller."

"But how, Stanko?"

"Listen, little one. The gift of telling fortunes is not all that it appears. It needs a quick wit, a keen eye, and a ready ear. Did I not teach Meg? Now is she known in the taverns and hamlets on the road as a Chosen One. Yes, you shall learn. We must begin our studies this very day."

After their woodland meal Stanko began his lessons. He sat on the steps of the van while Betty, from a log near by, attentively listened. Joe strolled away to inspect the camp.

When he returned some time later Betty and Stanko were still talking earnestly together. At Joe's approach Stanko rose. "Our first lesson is finished. Now shall we practise. Upon whom, little one?"

Betty looked gayly round. "Anyone, Stanko. I feel that I can tell any person's fortune."

Joe laughed scornfully. "You only think you can!"

"I know I can," Betty returned.

Joe gave her a keen glance. He was doubtful; but he saw that Betty really believed that she could do it.

"We'll let you try," Stanko remarked. "Boris!" he called. "Boris! Come here."

A youthful gypsy, black-eyed and black-haired, came over to the fire while the others indifferently looked on.

"The little one wishes to tell your fortune," continued the old man, with a sly wink. "Hold out your hand, Boris."

Boris smiled. "No one can tell my fortune— even Meg failed. And no one can compete with her."

"Oh, yes, I can," Betty said eagerly.

Joe drew nearer. If Betty really could tell fortunes, then they both might stay with the tribe. But could she do it? Would she really be able to win a place for them in the gypsy circle?

"Let me see, now," began Betty, taking Boris's hand. "You were born far away from here —across the sea."

"It is true. Go on."

"You lived, as a little boy, on the banks of a great river; it is called the Danube."

The dark young gypsy appeared nonplussed. "You told her?" he asked Stanko.

The old man shook his head. "Perhaps she is one of the Chosen Few. Go on, little one."

"You wish to marry a beautiful girl of the tribe, but you have not enough goatskins to please her father. Is it not true?"

"It is true, little one."

Joe's eyes widened in surprise. How did Betty know?

"She has a black temper, however," went on the little fortune teller; "and she will make you miserable. She will pull your hair and throw pots and pans——"

"Ah, I knew it!" shrieked the young gypsy. "I suspected that she was a shrew!" He waved his arms wildly and stormed up and down before the van. "The little one speaks the truth; she knows more than Meg herself!"

The other gypsies crowded about the little circle. "Call a traveler from the road," one of them suggested. "Let her tell a stranger's fortune."

"Yes, yes," the others echoed, "let her tell the fortune of a stranger. If she does as well, then will she belong to our tribe."

Joe looked on in great amazement. Had Stanko taught Betty so soon? Or was it a trick between

Betty and the old gypsy? He glanced at Stanko and caught a merry twinkle in his eyes.

Two of the gypsies ran to the roadside. Presently they came back dragging a beggar by the arm.

"But I am only a poor tinker," the miserable man whimpered. "Why do you clutch me in this unseemly manner?"

Joe looked at the bedraggled fellow. His clothes were worn and ragged; his hat was crownless; but what caught Joe's eye and held it was the man's strange face. It was bearded and half-hidden by a large black patch over the left eye.

"We only wish to tell your fortune, young sir," said Stanko kindly. "Let the little one see your palm."

The beggar reluctantly held out his hand. "No young chick can tell aught of me," he snickered. "I'm only Nat the Blinker o' Banbury. A tinker I be."

"You have walked far to-day," began Betty in a matter-of-fact tone. "You are on your way to Nottingham Fair and you go alone."

" 'Tis true, little sparrow."

"You go to shoot in the archery contest. Yet no one would think that you could shoot an arrow straight to the heart of the target."

"Never in my life have I been told such truths," said the beggar in a sarcastic tone.

At once the gypsies laughed loudly. "An archer, indeed! Try again, little one."

"Yet, it is true," continued Betty composedly, with a quick side glance at Stanko. "This man will win the Sheriff's prize, a golden arrow."

This was too much for the gypsies. They howled in mirth and slapped one another on the back as if this were the greatest joke they had heard for many a moon. The beggar also laughed, yet there was a puzzled expression on his face as he gazed at Betty. The little fortune teller's anger rose at the persistent ridicule of the crowd.

"Why do you all laugh?" she cried, stamping her foot. "Do you not know that I am speaking the truth?"

"It cannot be the truth, little friend," said Boris gently. "This man is only a tinker of the roads."

Betty's eyes flashed. "This man a tinker of the roads?" she scornfully cried. "Are you all blind? Next to the King he is the most famous man in all England! A price is upon his head. Every archer at the Fair is hoping to capture him!"

She stopped at the look of amazement upon the tinker's face. The gypsies had crowded about and now stood silent, puzzled.

"You mean——" began Boris.

"I mean that this man is disguised." She pointed at the tattered figure. "There stands Robin Hood, the outlaw of Sherwood Forest!"

III

Robin Hood in Disguise

IN THE moment of startled silence that followed, the tinker threw off his tattered hat, jerked the bandage from his eye, and suddenly drew himself to his full height.

"It is true," he said calmly. "This little sparrow has the keenest eye of anyone I have ever met. I am Robin Hood; yet here I know I am safe, for have I not ever been the friend of the people of the road?"

"True, true," chimed the circle. "Never would we give up the brave Robin to the cruelty of the Sheriff's men."

"Yet would I fight if needs be," cried Robin, stepping back and putting his hand on the knife that gleamed in his girdle.

Joe looked admiringly at the dauntless figure before him. The man's eyes shone with fire; his body was ready to spring if necessary; every muscle was taut. Surely a bold outlaw—this Robin Hood.

"Nay! Nay!" cried Stanko with a gesture for

quiet. "The outlaws of Sherwood Forest are ever welcome in a gypsy camp. Are not our enemies the same—the Sheriff who drives us off the commons, the wealthy barons and knights who crowd us from the highways? Our home is the open road, with the grass for a bed and the stars for a blanket. Nay, Robin, resume your disguise. None shall tell."

"None shall tell," echoed the circle.

"Thanks, my merry Romanys," said Robin as he replaced the patch over his left eye. "I knew I was among friends. Truly you have a most marvelous soothsayer here."

Betty blushed, then she said softly: "I have heard much of you, sir. How could anyone mistake Robin Hood!"

"By St. Dunstan, young miss, you should be telling fortunes at the Fair." He picked up his hat. "Good-bye, good friends. I go to take the golden arrow from beneath the Sheriff's nose." He wheeled and with a long swinging stride went down the hill toward the gleaming tents.

Betty jumped from the steps as the little crowd dispersed. "Now I can tell fortunes at the Fair, can't I, Stanko?" she asked.

"You must, little one," said the gypsy approvingly. "I am beginning to believe that you are really a Chosen One. A tent all your own shall we put up near the shooting match. It shall be decked with ribbons and bunting fit for a queen of the gypsies."

"Yes, I'll be a gypsy queen, a gypsy queen!" She skipped about in rapture.

Joe gave a contemptuous shrug. "I don't think I'd ask you to tell my fortune," he remarked. "I'd rather see the shooting match."

"Who asked you for your opinion, Master Joey?" Betty retorted. "I shall probably be too busy, anyway, speaking to the barons and their ladies."

Joe placidly stirred the fire. Through the corner of his eye he watched Betty adorn herself with gay shawls and ribbons, and when Stanko and Boris led the way to the meadow to set up a small red tent for her, he followed. He didn't care about the tent, he told himself; but he did want to see the archery contest.

When he reached the Fair grounds Joe found himself lost in a maze of tents where the people of the countryside jostled each other, all laughing and throwing friendly jests and pleasantries. Peasants, leading goats and pigs, elbowed their way in the crowd. Long-horned cattle, that had come all the way from Spain, gazed lazily at the spectators. Through the throng peddlers loudly hawked their wares of beads and silks, carried on trays upheld by cords around their shoulders.

Three silver notes of a bugle sounded, and Joe was swept with the populace toward the shooting match. A long open runway with a target at the far end served as the gallery; the townspeople thronged one side, while opposite stood the gayly decked stands wherein sat the Sheriff and the knights and barons with their ladies fair.

The Sheriff, with a dignified attitude, lifted his hand. The bugle again sounded three notes. It was the signal, and the match began.

Joe, who had edged to the front, saw that at least ten men were competing. Among them was the ragged tinker—Robin Hood. This number, however, was soon reduced by bad shots, until only two were left—a brawny blacksmith called Hugh o' the Moors and the penniless tinker of the roads.

The crowd now took sides. Some shouted for the tattered stranger, and others for Hugh o' the Moors. The latter took up his bow and, after taking careful aim, lodged an arrow straight in the heart of the target. The onlookers applauded with shouts and cheers.

"By St. Hubert, that was a shot!"

"The smith wins!"

"The ragged robin cannot better that!"

The one-eyed archer lifted his bow with seeming carelessness and let fly the shaft. The spectators gasped. Hugh's missile fell broken to the ground, and in its place quivered the stranger's arrow.

"The ragged robin wins! The stranger wins!" shouted the multitude.

With cheers and cries of admiration they dragged the victor before the high seat of the Sheriff.

"Brave archer," said the Sheriff, rising to his feet and coming forward to the edge of the stand, "here is the prize you have fairly won. What is your name and whence do you hail?"

"From Banbury I come," replied the tinker. "Nat the Blinker am I called."

"Well, Nat, for a man who blinks with only one eye, you shoot marvelously straight."

Joe at that moment felt someone pulling at his arm. "Oh, Joe," Betty gasped in a whisper, "I've told a dozen fortunes already—and everyone says I've told wonderful truths!"

Joe shrugged. "Listen to the Sheriff."

The Sheriff turned to his wife. "Did you speak, Dame Millicent?" he asked; but she shook her head. He paused and glanced at the baron on his right. Someone said: "But it can't be true!"

"Oh, I knew it!" murmured Betty in Joe's ear. "Somebody has recognized Robin!"

*The one-eyed archer lifted his bow with seeming care-
lessness and let fly the shaft*

The Sheriff stared with keen eyes at the tinker. "You say you are Nat the Blinker," he continued with sudden understanding in his voice; "yet one of my guardsmen tells me you are not!"

The crowd stood breathless. This was more than it had been led to expect. Joe saw the tinker's hand stealthily creep up to his girdle. The action was evidently noticed by the Sheriff as well. He raised his arms in a gesture of rage and indignation.

"Seize him, men!" he cried. "He is Robin Hood himself!"

With a sudden leap Robin flung himself into the sea of people.

At once the great meadow was plunged into an uproar. Shouts for the King's soldiery were mingled with the shrieks of women and the calls of men. Like the great swell of a heavy sea, the multitude swayed backward and forward while the noise and hubbub rose to a deafening clamor.

"Hunt for him! Find him!" shouted the Sheriff in a frenzy. "Robin Hood must not escape this time!"

IV

Flight!

THE gypsy fires were glowing in the dusk as Betty and Joe, tired and breathless, reached the camp on the hillside.

"My tent's gone, Stanko!" quavered Betty as she came up to the old man near the fire. "The crowd knocked it down and walked all over it!" She was near to tears.

"That matters not, little one," Stanko answered. "Only for you was I worried; I lost you in the throng." He stirred a steaming kettle hanging from a tripod above the fire. "We need wood, Joe," he suggested. "Get the ax from the van."

Joe eagerly mounted the steps at the back of the green van. On the threshold of the open door he paused, startled.

"Robin Hood!" Joe stood open-mouthed. "How—how did you get here?"

"Robin Hood!" exclaimed Betty. She came running with a spoon in her hand. At the top of the steps she, too, paused in amazement. "Oh, Stanko!"

Within the van, unconcernedly seated upon a box, was Robin Hood. His tattered hat and black eyepiece had been removed; a pair of alert blue eyes twinkled at the three who faced him from the doorway.

"Where should I go for safety," he asked, "if not to the camp of my friends the Romanys?"

Stanko nodded. "Ah, Robin, you are safe," he answered. "For that am I thankful. Yet I fear your presence here may bring trouble upon the tribe. Even now the Sheriff's men scour the countryside for you."

Robin resumed his tattered hat. "Then will I go, Stanko my friend, before the soldiers arrive." He rose and fingered the knife in his girdle.

Betty clutched the old gypsy's arm. "You wouldn't turn him out, Stanko—out to be captured by the King's men!" she pleaded.

Stanko looked warily round. "Have we not been helped many times by the outlaws of Sherwood Forest? No, we shall hide him within this very van!"

He entered the small interior and pointed to a ring in the flooring. "See—there is a false bottom in the floor where I keep valuables. It is not very large, but I know Robin can squeeze within if necessary."

Joe pulled back the white curtain from the tiny

window and gazed through the deepening twilight toward the meadow. The people of the Fair were scattering in groups of three and four, some to the town and others to the cottages among the purple hills. Soldiers were beating the thickets on the edge of the slope, where juniper berries hung in great blue clusters.

"They're coming—soldiers!—two of them," Joe warned in an excited whisper.

Swift as a hawk, Robin crossed to the window. "They're searching the wagons," he murmured.

"Quick! Hide, Robin!" cried Betty.

While Stanko and Betty helped Robin into his hiding place Joe kept watch at the window. The two soldiers were making a systematic search of the gypsy camp, peering into tents and vans, searching dark corners, and flinging aside the inquisitive children. They were at the blue van.

"Sit out on the steps, little one," whispered Stanko.

When the soldiers reached the green van everything was orderly and quiet. The old gypsy stirred the stew; Joe tended the fire; Betty sat in an attitude of indifference on the steps.

"By holy St. Dunstan," said one of the soldiers as he critically surveyed the interior of the van, "I believe he has escaped us! This is the last one and 'tis empty."

" 'Tis strange these people of the road be here," remarked the other; "for the Sheriff likes not gypsies near Nottingham Town."

When the two soldiers at last departed Betty's eyes sparkled with triumph.

"Not a word," warned Stanko. "Eat as usual."

"And leave Robin in that tight place with his nose pressed against the floor?"

" 'Twill be better than the Sheriff's noose," returned the gypsy; "though I fear we should be up and away, for sheriffs are ever prone to vent their anger upon those who cannot bite back."

While they were eating their supper of grilled partridge and black bread, an abrupt crackling noise in the thicket near by drew their attention. They turned to see Boris emerge from the gloom of the trees.

"Make ready!" he cried with labored breath. "The Sheriff believes we are hiding Robin Hood! His men prepare to destroy the camp!"

Horrified, Joe and Betty gazed toward the meadow, now lying black and silent in the late evening. Slowly, deliberately coming up the slope toward them was a company of foot soldiers, lighting their way with flaring torches. Ever swelling in volume rose the low measured chant of their war song.

"Fly! Fly for your lives!" shrieked a withered hag.

The others took up the cry. "Away—away—away! To Sherwood Forest! To Locksley Town!"

Gypsies, beggars, vagabonds, and people of the road are always poised for flight; and Stanko's tribe was no exception. Amid shouts and frantic calls tents were leveled, ponies harnessed, carts loaded, doors closed.

One van, quicker than the others, swung through the camp and clattered down the dark highway. Flames from the camp fires shone like molten gold on the green and yellow wagons. Dogs barked as they scampered about the wheels; horses stamped and impatiently pawed the ground.

Away! Away to Sherwood Forest! Thundering hoofs on the rutted road; swaying, creaking vans plunging into the blackness; cracking whips urging the horses onward.

"Into the van, little one! Into the van, Joe! I drive to-night!"

A sudden turn that threw them toward the window; the swelling volume of the hue and cry; the last gleam of the camp fire lighting up the dim interior; the rocking wheels and the galloping horses; and someone shouting, "Stop that van! Stop that——"

Then the even swing on the great black highway, with the wind racing by and the vans plunging on toward Sherwood.

V

The Golden Arrow

M IMO and Zulieka are getting tired," said Joe. "They're slowing down now."

He sat inside the van upon the bench beneath the window, looking out at the dark trees flying past. The moon had risen and from a star-dimmed heaven sent a silver glow across the hills. One ray fell upon Betty where she sat opposite.

"Poor Robin," she whispered. "Oh, it must be safe now. We'll let him out, Joe."

She was down on her knees, searching for the ring in the flooring. "Hurry, Joe; help me!"

They jerked at the trap door, and like a jack-in-the-box up sat Robin Hood. He made a wry face as he rubbed his head.

"Are you hurt?" asked Betty.

"Oh, no," he sighed; "but it wasn't exactly comfortable in there." He smiled. "It saved me, and for that I have you to thank."

He rose and glanced from the window. "We've

48

reached Sherwood. Stop, Stanko; let me out."

The ponies slowed down to a canter, then to a walk. "Whoa, Mimo. Whoa, Zulieka," commanded the gypsy.

Robin Hood jumped to the ground. "I do not hear the pursuit," he said. "They must have given up the chase."

"Must you leave us here, Robin?"

"My men will be looking for me." He took a small bugle from his ragged garments and sounded a long, clear blast.

Almost immediately a horn far in the depths of the greenwood answered. "'Tis my friends Will Scarlet and Friar Tuck, I doubt not." He handed to Stanko a glistening object. "This, the Sheriff's golden arrow, I give to you three—the People of the Green Van who to-night so boldly proved their friendship. . . . Good-bye, Stanko; good-bye, little friends!"

He turned and as noiseless as the shadow of a passing cloud, strode off into the gloom of the forest. Betty and Joe waved after him.

Stanko again took up the reins. "On, Mimo! On, Zulieka! We must hurry to meet the caravan." He looked at the two children, who had climbed up beside him. "We make camp soon. You may sit here, though I nod when we travel of nights."

"That wonderful golden arrow," Betty began. "What shall we do with it?"

"Keep it, of course," said Joe. "It belongs to the van; we might tack it above the door."

"It's not a horseshoe, silly."

Stanko chuckled. "For safe keeping, little ones, I think we might put it in the chest beneath the floor."

"The very place!" agreed Betty.

Stanko dozed at the reins as the ponies trotted along the moonlit road. He roused himself to say: "You have won your place in the tribe by your fortune telling, little one."

"I'm so happy," breathed Betty.

Joe gave her a quick glance. "Was it real?" he asked.

"Of course it was!"

"But how did you do it, Betty?—how did you know Robin?"

"I looked at his hand."

Joe was incredulous. "And that told you?" he asked.

"Partly. You see it was like this: Stanko said to watch people carefully—to be observant! First I saw that the tinker's hand wasn't black and hard like a tinker's. Then when he looked down at me his eye bandage dropped a tiny bit to one side—and I saw that the eye back of it was looking, too! I glanced at Stanko, and he was trying not to laugh. He knew that man! And remembering Alan-a-Dale and his story of Robin in disguise, I thought I'd chance it—but I wasn't sure! Not till the very last!"

The old gypsy laughed softly. "It was cleverly done, little one. Meg shall teach you more. There is much to learn. . . . But was it not a wonderful adventure?"

She clasped her hands. "It was wonderful, Stanko!" And Joe, for once, agreed.

"Who knows," mused the gypsy, "what adventures may await us on the road to-morrow!"

Betty and Joe nodded sleepily as the van wound over the moonlit hills.

"*I sing a song of a troubadour*
As he sings to his lady love;
I sing a gay romance of yore
As old as the stars above. . . ."
BLONDEL'S SONG

I

Toto the Bear

WHOA, Mimo! Whoa, Zulieka!" Stanko, the Gypsy dropped the reins of the two ponies. "Can you read the road sign, little ones?"

Both Betty and Joe jumped to the ground, but Betty was the quicker. "The arrow points ahead, Stanko," she called; "and the sign says:

TO

THE ENGLISH CHANNEL

FRANCE AND AUSTRIA.

Gracious! Are we going across the sea?"

Stanko nodded. "These be troublous times in England with the great King Richard absent on the Holy Crusade. Now that winter approaches, 'tis well for us to go south to the land of the Romanys in the Danube Valley. But we shall return with the wild geese when the sun moves northward."

"On a real boat?" cried Joe.

"A beautiful ship with sails like a great white bird. Jump up, little master. On, Mimo! On, Zulieka! On to Dover!"

Moored to the wharves lay the Dover boats with their tall masts and furled sails rising white against the sea-blue sky. Stanko's tribe had already boarded one of the ships, and the green van was the last to be put aboard. What thrilling fun it was! Breathlessly Betty watched their ponies being slowly led to the deck where the gypsy caravan was crowded. The tribe was merry at the thought of journeying toward its Southern home.

Betty leaned against the rail, watching the sailors make ready to cast off. Her hand touched a shaggy object. She turned in sharp surprise.

Standing on its hind legs and unconcernedly gazing shoreward was a black bear. He had straight heavy fur and he was twice as tall as Betty.

"Oh, a bear!" she cried. "Joe, look at the bear."

"He's tame, of course," Joe pronounced. "See, he has a ring in his nose and a chain."

A white-haired gypsy held the bear's chain. The old man now came over to them. "Don't be afraid," he said; "Toto likes children."

"Likes them!" Betty murmured. "Does he eat them?"

"Ho, ho! Toto is the friend of all the children. He dances for them while I collect the pennies."

With his huge mouth set in a friendly grin, Toto lumbered across the deck.

"Does he always walk on his hind legs?"

"Of course. Toto is proud that he can walk as men do and not as common bears."

Toto now evidently thought it time to show his tricks to the interested spectators. In his clumsy fashion he began to hop about.

"He wishes to dance for you," explained the old gypsy. "Dance, Toto! Dance for the small folk."

The gypsy struck up a gay little tune on a tiny whistle, and the bear at once began to dance. He swung backward and forward in short ungainly steps while his shaggy forepaws clawed the air. His huge body swayed to the rhythm of the lilting melody; his mouth hung open in joyous abandon.

A circle had formed about the bear, and now

all the gypsies began to applaud and laugh at his awkward antics. Toto soon stopped and bowed; then he went round the circle as if silently asking for pennies.

"No, Toto! No!" his owner cried. "These be Romany folk like us. Only the *gorgios* pay pennies."

Toto and his admirers were brushed aside as the brawny sailors came forward. To the sound of chanteis sung in sharp quick beats, they dragged up the anchor.

"Spread sail!" ordered the Captain.

At that moment a shout from the receding wharf carried Betty and the passengers to the rail. Toto took his place there, too. Running toward them down the wharf was a man in brilliant dress.

"Wait! Wait!" he shouted. "I must cross to Calais with you; I go through France to Austria!"

The stranger rushed to the wharf's edge and stood there looking across the widening distance.

"Who are you?" the Captain demanded.

"I am Blondel," came back the answer. "Blondel, troubadour to Richard the Lion-Hearted!"

II

The Troubadour Blondel

THE passengers stirred audibly. "Blondel! Blondel!" they murmured. "The great troubadour of Richard of England."

A boat was lowered, and a few minutes later Blondel climbed up the ladder to the deck. Betty thought she had never before seen such glorious clothes and brilliant colors. They were gold and blue, puffed with lace here, tied with ribbon there. Over the troubadour's shoulder was slung a lute suspended by golden cords.

"Why do you hurry to Austria?" demanded the Captain.

Blondel bowed his head; his voice was low. "Because Richard the Lion-Hearted is a prisoner."

"A prisoner!" Murmurs of surprise and dismay went round the circle.

"Yes, Richard of England is a prisoner! . . . You know how proudly he led his mighty army on the Crusade against the Infidel. You know how bravely he battered at the gates of Jerusalem till the Holy City fell beneath his onslaught. His duty then being over, he had but one thought —to return to his beloved England. He wished to travel the straightest road, the swiftest road; and that led through Austria, the land of his enemy.

"Richard has the heart of a lion; he fears nothing. He sent his ships and his men and his goods by the long sea route, while he entered Austria disguised."

Blondel paused. Betty edged nearer; the circle whispered in awe.

"He dared to enter Austria!"

"Oh, a foolhardy trick. But a brave one!"

"Only Richard the Lion-Hearted would have chosen the short road home."

"In Austria his disguise was discovered," Blondel went on sadly. "He was captured. Duke Leopold the Austrian is his mortal enemy. Now the Duke hides our valiant heart in some dark dungeon to weep in vain for England."

"But our armies shall free him!" said the Captain. "Where is he hidden?"

"No one knows. Austria is a broad land and we know not which castle to storm. Our armies are upon the sea and 'twill be months before they reach London. Could we find this hiding place we might ransom him—buy his freedom with gold and jewels before he dies in black despair."

"And you? You go to Austria alone in quest of him?"

Blondel threw back his head; his eyes flashed in the evening sun. "Yes, I go to search for Richard. A troubadour is ever welcome at inn and wayside tavern, and there mayhap I shall hear gossip. Richard's hidden prison must be found."

"Yes, it must be found!" echoed the Captain.

"It was Alan-a-Dale who told me that a gypsy tribe journeyed southward. I knew that with the Romanys I could reach the Danube Valley."

"You are welcome, Blondel," said Stanko. "Were Richard in England now there would not be need of locked doors at night. Come, you sup with the Romanys."

Betty turned to the rail. Already the white coast of England was dipping into the sea. A breath of wind caressed her cheek. Toto also came lumbering to the rail where he snuffed the air. Abruptly he dropped on all fours to the deck.

"You told me he never walked like a bear," remarked Betty to his owner. "Now look at him."

"Toto scents a storm," the gypsy explained. "The sky is darkening."

Betty saw that it was true. The ship was

heading toward a black cloud that seemed to be closing down upon the heaving ocean.

"Everybody below!" the Captain shouted. "A storm approaches. Lash the sails, my hearties! Tie down the wagons!"

Betty was one of the last to descend the hatchway into the ship's hold. Blondel stood alone at the rail with his eyes fixed upon the thin line that was England.

"Below, Blondel!" commanded the Captain.

"I wish to remain above. Perhaps I should like to write a poem about the storm."

"Below, fool! Were Richard himself aboard he would obey the Captain of the Ship."

"But I am Blondel the Poet."

The Captain gave a gesture of dismissal. "Stay then if you will, but blame me not if a wave should wash you overboard."

Below deck Betty found two lighted lanterns hanging from the cross beams. The gypsies curled themselves up for the night on the bales of cargo. Joe took his place near Toto the Bear. Betty, however, could not sleep. The wind bellowed about the ship and the waves pounded the deck. It seemed hours later when she suddenly raised her head, startled.

Above the wind and rain a dull crash thudded overhead.

She leaned on one elbow and listened. Hands were dragging at the closed hatch. A flash of lightning revealed the ladder; she saw two sailors lifting down the limp form of the troubadour, Blondel. His gay suit was wet and bedraggled. The men left their charge at the bottom of the ladder. Betty heard the injured man mutter in pain.

She saw that no one stirred. Quietly she rose and picked her way across the crowded space to the troubadour's side.

"You are hurt?" she whispered.

He moaned faintly. "The topgallant fell. It caught my foot. Oh, it's broken—broken! How shall I get to Austria now!"

"Broken?" She was all pity. "You must tie it up, then. Look, I will help you."

"Now will I have to remain in Calais while the tribe goes on without me. Oh, I was a fool to stay on deck."

"Yes, you should have come down with us. There! Does that hurt less?"

Blondel smiled his thanks. "Your hand is as light as a wind-blown petal. . . . The pain is gone, but the ache about my heart remains. Oh, Richard—Richard of England! Who can search for you now? Who can find your secret prison in Austria?"

"Is there no one left?"

Blondel groaned in remorse and contrition. "No one. It must be stealthily done. I had planned to journey up and down the Danube Valley, singing my songs to the people of Austria. I hoped to hear a whisper, perhaps just a breath of gossip about some great lord kept in a dungeon. But I would know—I would have found my King's hiding place. And now——"

"If I could help——" Betty began.

"You are so little—so little." But Blondel's eyes gleamed. "Perhaps—perhaps because you are so small no one would suspect. . . . Yes! You can help! You must!"

"But how, Blondel? How?"

He glanced furtively about. In the gloom the two bronze lanterns swung slowly to and fro. They cast a pale light upon the huddled forms of the sleeping gypsies. Not a soul stirred. Blondel leaned closer.

"Listen, little one. We shall save Richard yet —you and I! Can you sing? Yes? Then shall I teach you Richard's favorite song. It goes thus:

> *"I sing a song of a troubadour*
> *As he sings to his lady love;*
> *I sing a gay romance of yore*
> *As old as the stars above. . . .*

Is it not a pretty air?"

"It is beautiful, Blondel."

"Then shall you take this song throughout the broad land of Austria. If you see a dark tower against the sky, there shall you sing this song! If you hear of a dungeon black and deep, there shall you sing this song! Richard will hear and give you a sign."

"A sign, Blondel? What do you mean?"

"Richard will let you know. He will give you some token—perhaps a ring or a jewel. See him yourself. See if he is well. Send the token and the name of the prison to England by the swiftest rider of the tribe. I shall be waiting at the Dover boat."

"How shall I sing this song in Austria— alone?"

Blondel spoke eagerly. "It is not difficult. Do not the gypsies follow the open road? Listen! You shall sing Richard's song as I had planned to sing it—in the courtyard of the caravansaries where travelers stop. You will need help. If Toto and the boy . . . Yes, I shall pay old white-beard to lend the bear to you and the boy. Toto will dance while you sing to the people of Austria. Let ever your eyes search the windows of the castles for a sign. Richard's heart will nigh burst with joy when he hears your song. Let him know that England waits for his return. . . . See, the

dawn is here! Look out the port and tell me:
Do you see England?"

Betty moved quietly across to the tiny port-
hole. "Only the waves and a single star," she
whispered.

"Richard loved that land," Blondel sighed.
"You will go in quest of this brave heart of
ours?"

"I promise, Blondel. . . . Now, how goes that
song?"

III

Whispers in the Market Place

BETTY opened the van door and paused on the steps to gaze about. The dew lay heavy upon the grass. Through the trees she saw the Danube flowing down through Austria to the sea. The tang of wood smoke mingled with the tantalizing odor of frying bacon.

"Ho, little one!" greeted Stanko. "You are not up with the larks this morning. Breakfast is ready."

"I'm hungry, too, Stanko. Where's Joe?"

"He's feeding Toto. That bear follows him like a pet lamb."

Joe soon appeared with Toto, who seated himself near by while they ate.

"Where do we go this morning, Betty?" Joe asked.

"First to Gratz." Betty looked southward where, on a rise above the river, the town lay framed in its high stone wall.

"To-day is market day," she resumed; "and we may hear news."

"News—news!" Joe retorted. "It's five weeks since we started with Toto to hunt for the place where Richard is hidden. We never hear anything; we never will. Richard the Lion-Hearted——"

"Hush, Joe!" Betty held up a warning hand. "Someone might hear."

"But we never hear anything," blurted Joe.

"Shame, lad!" Stanko set down his dish of porridge. "Has not the little one courageously walked and sung for the one hope—to get news? And now would you dishearten her?"

Betty's eyes shone with unshed tears. "I won't be discouraged. I won't! Perhaps this very morning we'll hear of him."

"Perhaps," Joe murmured.

They set out for the town in better spirits, for Joe never tired of Toto and his tricks. At the great North Gate of Gratz a guard glanced at them carelessly and let them pass. Through the winding, cobbled streets they went, beneath jutting houses that whispered together overhead. Toto, dancing in his clumsy way, sent the children of the town into ecstatic joy. After Joe had collected a few pennies they moved on to the next corner.

In the Market Place they found the peasants

of the countryside gathered about their produce. Cabbages and carrots, sausages and cheese, woven cloths and beads were spread on the open square. A crowd soon surrounded the little troupe.

Betty at once began her song, a gypsy air that Stanko had taught her, a song as old as the gypsies themselves. Toto followed next with his tricks. To the gleeful shouts of the throng the bear danced, while Betty strummed on her mandolin. It was not extraordinary music; even Betty admitted that, but it served as an accompaniment to Toto's efforts. Toto, at least, was pleased; he always waited till Betty began and always ended his dance with her last touch of the strings.

When the bear had finished Betty turned to the crowd and said: "Listen, People of Gratz! Now will I sing for you a song of far-off England, a song taught me by a Pilgrim who journeyed with us Romanys toward the Holy Land. It is not many singers who can sing a song of England."

"True! True!" agreed the circle. "Surely this little singer is doubly learnèd for one of her age. Listen to the foreign song."

Betty strummed upon the strings and began Blondel's song:

I sing a song of a troub-a-dour As he sings to his la _ dy love, I sing a gay ro - mance of yore, As __ old as the stars a - bove. My song is plain - tive, my song is sad; This __ song that I sing __ to thee Be-neath the skies of South-ern lands: Where is Rich-ard of Brit - tan - y? Be - neath the skies of South-ern lands, O __ Rich-ard of Brit-tan _ y!

The circle listened in wonderment to this ballad from the strange land beyond the sea. They knew not the words, but the lilting melody held them. When the song ended they broke into prolonged applause.

One tall fellow dressed as a cook emerged from the doorway of a near-by tavern and came toward them. "An English song, say you? I did serve, three months gone by, a man who mentioned this country of England."

In sudden hope, Betty stared at him. "An Englishman?"

The cook shook his head. "I know not. But one night when a storm roared up the Danube Valley travelers put into our tavern for shelter. One was a prisoner who sat apart, his chains clanking on the floor. I was angry at serving them at that hour of the night, but they paid well."

"Yes, and who mentioned England?"

"It was the prisoner. When I put down as fine a sausage as mortal man could ever wish he pushed it aside, saying: 'In England it would be roast mutton that I'd call for.' His captors turned upon him, saying: 'Mention not that country! Never shall you see it again!'"

Betty listened with breathless interest. After all these weeks of vain search for a clue she could hardly believe this good fortune. Perhaps this prisoner was Richard!

"Yes, and then what?" she asked.

"The man appeared much downcast," continued the cook. "He sat hunched in his chair and hardly touched the food before him. I heard him murmur: 'England—England!'"

"Which way did they go?" Betty asked.

"Not far, I think, for one of the men I knew. He lives near by. . . . But I have talked too much already." He turned and disappeared through the tavern door.

Betty wanted to shout the tidings to Joe, who was putting Toto through his tricks; but she knew that caution was needed. She sang one more gypsy air before they moved on.

As they crossed the thronged Market Place she whispered: "Joe, do you remember what Blondel said? *If you hear of a dungeon dark and deep, there shall you sing this song!*"

"Yes," Joe drearily replied, "we've sung near every prison in Austria, and we haven't yet heard a word of Richard."

Betty laughed softly. "Do you remember what else he said? *If you see a tall tower dark against the sky, there shall you sing this song.*"

"And haven't we sung beneath every tower in Austria?"

"But not this one."

"Which one?"

Joe followed her gaze across the housetops of the Market Place. Against the clear blue of the Southern sky crouched a gray pile of stone; and raising its head toward the heavens, with its two high windows blinking in the sun, a dark tower beckoned toward them.

IV
The Tower of Gratz

THE late afternoon sun painted the Castle of Gratz, perched on its somber cliff above the river, with splashes of deep wine red. As the shadows climbed the town wall three strolling players wandered up the street to the huge fortress. Here and there the girl sang; then the boy collected pennies while the bear danced.

The gates of the Castle were closed. On the rampart above, a lone guard paced back and forth.

"Sing, Betty," whispered Joe.

At once Betty, strumming her mandolin, sang her gypsy melody. The guard paused in his march and gazed down upon the strange trio.

"Bravo!" he shouted when she had finished. "'Tis a pretty air, little singer."

"Now watch the bear!" Joe called. "Dance, Toto! Dance for the guardsman!"

At the sound of Betty's playing Toto began his ungainly waltz.

TOWER OF GRATZ

The guardsman laughed in high glee. "A jolly bear!" he shouted. "I would that you might enter the courtyard to cheer a little this gloomy pile."

"Toto has many other tricks."

The guardsman looked about him for a moment; then, leaning far over the wall, he said in a lowered voice: "The Baron is away. I will descend to the gate."

The three crossed the wooden drawbridge which spanned the black water of the moat. The great iron-studded gate did not open to them, however; a small doorway at one side drew back. "Step through, little players," whispered the guardsman with a frightened glance up and down the street. "It is many moons since a song was heard in the Tower of Gratz."

Within the courtyard moss grew thick about the flagstones; it clung to the Castle walls as if the sun seldom dared venture into that dreary confine. A low murmur came from a door leading down into a candle-lighted cellar; the Baron's henchmen were evidently at their evening meal.

"Begin, little singer," said the guardsman. "You will soon bring the garrison racing up the stairs to hear your music."

The gypsy song brought a swift patter of feet on the stairway. "A singer!" a voice cried. "And a bear!"

"Dance, Toto!" ordered Joe.

The kitchen maids shouted with glee as Toto swayed to the music. In a circle about the trio were gathered men and women, laughing, applauding, their eyes sparkling at this unexpected pleasure.

"Have you eaten, little folks?" asked a maid. "No? Then shall you sup with us. To the cellar, everyone! They will entertain us after meal time."

"Not yet," Betty hurriedly interrupted. "Let me sing one song first. I never can sing after eating, and I am hungry to-night. Listen! This is a song of a land far away."

"Italy or Spain, perhaps," remarked a guardsman.

"Perhaps," answered Betty, then began:

> "*I sing a song of a troubadour*
> *As he sings to his lady love . . .*"

Her voice thrilled like a bell far out over the tops of the Castle walls. A hush stole upon the shadowy courtyard; the ramparts seemed to listen expectantly, the tower to bend its head in amazed disbelief.

The company applauded roundly and turned to the kitchen. Joe and Toto rushed with the others down the stairway, but Betty slipped away unseen toward a corner of the gray wall.

Before her the tower, soaring up to heaven, flamed like a torch in the evening air. She listened; again the battlements listened, too. The purple shadows crept higher till only the topmost window shot back the sunlight. Softly from high up in the tower a voice answered her serenade.

A sign—a sign! The words floated down deep and clear:

> *"I sing a gay romance of yore*
> *As old as the stars above . . ."*

With rapt attention—with her eyes fixed on a window far above—she listened. Blondel's song! Her very own song! She pressed her hands together in ecstasy.

In mid-air something glittered for a second in the sunset glow. A light tinkle sounded on the flagstones at her feet. Trembling with eagerness, she reached down and picked up a heavy ring of beaten gold. She hardly dared to believe her eyes.

Engraved upon it was a couchant leopard—the seal of Richard the Lion-Hearted!

V

The Captive Leopard

WHAT a bear! What a manlike bear! Draw another bench, Franz, and let Toto eat at the table."

Around the long, candle-lighted table the company was seated. At its head in the seat of honor sat Toto, greatly enjoying his meal in the Baron's scullery. A huge platter of meat lay before him; he pounded the table with his two front paws.

With throbbing heart Betty slipped into the room. Timidly she advanced to the bench and seated herself next to a buxom maid, who loudly ordered another plate. Did the woman notice her excitement? How her hands trembled; how her lips quivered! She must take courage. These people must not suspect that she knew the name of their prisoner.

"Eat, my dearie, before the kettle is empty," said the woman. "The Baron's larder is never too well filled when the armies fight in Palestine."

Betty noted how the tipsy men and the loud-voiced women hung on Joe's stories about Toto; how they shrieked in mirth when he told how Toto had chased a thieving beggar. She saw Franz rise and take another plate, which he filled with stew. It was the great ring of keys upon his belt that drew her attention. Did he act as jailor to the prisoner in the tower?

"I go to feed my lord of the closed mouth," he explained to Joe. "He's locked in our bird cage."

"A prisoner?"

"Some petty landholder, I doubt not, whom my lord the Baron dislikes. The man is a silent fellow, morose and black-browed."

Betty's hands gripped the bench. Morose and black-browed! How could Richard the Lion-Hearted, who loved the roads and fields and forests, be otherwise when penned in a small dark prison!

With a candle lighted from the fireplace, Franz strode to a stairway at the end of the scullery. With sudden decision Betty whispered to her neighbor: "I don't feel well in this stuffy cellar. We've walked a long way to-day in the hot sun."

The woman absent-mindedly nodded. Betty rose and went to the stairway by which she had entered. There, with fast-beating heart, she turned. The company below were chattering like magpies on a roof; their glances were centered upon Toto. Betty slipped along the soot-stained wall to the second stairway, up which Franz had disappeared. Swiftly as an arrow she darted after him.

She found herself in a dusky hall with a raftered ceiling mistily fading into the gloom. Opposite her Franz was opening a small wooden door. She saw him pull at a thong, then bend his head as he went through. The door clicked shut behind him.

Betty crossed the hall and put her ear to the wooden panel. Not a sound came from within. Gaining courage, she reached for the latchstring and pulled it down. With a faint click the door swung ajar. As she entered the small dark room the musty odor of stagnant air assailed her nostrils in sickening waves. She discerned in one corner of the empty room a circular staircase leading up into black obscurity. She listened intently. Faint footfalls above told her that Franz was ascending the tower of Gratz.

By means of a second thong she noiselessly closed the door behind her. She was now in complete darkness, as though she were in a tomb far beneath the ground. Edging along the wall, she found the stairs and began to climb. The winding stairway was so narrow that she touched cold damp walls with each hand. Only the faint footsteps of Franz far above broke the profound silence.

A sudden scurrying about her feet made her cling to the wall in terror. She saw small evil eyes glowing like points of fire in the blackness. The tower rats were out! They were above her now, scampering up the stairs. One hand flew to her breast in horror. But she couldn't go back after all these months; somehow she must get word to Richard.

She closed her eyes to shut out the vision of those demon faces. Shrill squeals caught her ears. Panic seized her. She crouched against the stones.

Her thoughts raced to the kitchen. It was warm there, and the voices were friendly. Joe across the table, Toto at the head. Lights and laughter, food and drink! And here—here were crawling, creeping things in a dank prison. But Richard the Lion-Hearted was above. *He* wouldn't be afraid.

She continued upward. The cold slimy walls made her shudder. On she went, driving herself with one thought—Richard.

She must be high in the tower now, for it seemed to her she had climbed for hours. Suddenly a breath of clean air made her stop. A square window opened at her right hand. She leaned over the thick stone casing, inhaling gratefully the fresh cool air. Stars shone dimly overhead; a crescent moon hung low over the roofs of the town. She saw the glow of gypsy fires in the grove along the river. As she turned to continue her climb she glimpsed, in the pale light, a niche in the wall where a shelf held the figure of a saint. Prisoners, perhaps, were given leave to ask a prayer before being led to the cages above.

The muffled clanking of iron sent her hurrying upward. She had nearly reached the top. The distant voice of Franz floated down.

"Supper, my tongueless lord. Why do you not reach for it?"

Then came another voice low and vibrant: "Who sings to-night in the Castle yard? My lord of Austria returns?"

"Oh, ho! So you can talk! 'Twas only some strolling gypsies who happened by the town."

"A troubadour perhaps with a silver lute?"

"Not at all! These be little folk with a dancing bear. Never have I seen their like before! . . . Happy dreams, my lord."

Footfalls coming down the stairs! Betty wheeled and retraced her steps with breathless speed. At the window the niche caught her eye. Beneath the shelf it was dark and friendly. Cautiously the girl crept into this nook, where she crouched with pounding heart.

The footsteps drew nearer. A flicker of candle-light pierced the blackness. With jangling keys the jailor rounded the curve. He paused for a second to glance from the window, then passed on down the steps.

A rat scurried up the stairs. Betty wondered if it had smelled the food. She followed. At the top of the stairway a small barred window was out-lined against a candle-lighted room. Trembling with emotion, she stood on tiptoe to look within.

But it was not the King who awaited her there; it was a lonely, homesick man, shut away from the world he loved.

He moved back and forth with the stealthy tread of a caged beast, a chain on his ankle clank-ing at every turn. Abruptly stopping, he looked toward the door. Betty saw that his face was set like a mask. Only the eyes were alive. They glowed like fireflies from a misty hedge, darting here and there in sudden sharp movements.

"Who's there?" he whispered in a vibrant voice. "Who stands at the door? Is it you, Blondel?"

Betty opened her lips to speak, but the words refused to come. This man before her was King of England—Richard the Lion-Hearted. He was the hero of a nation; he was the leader of Europe's warriors. Twenty armies followed him to battle; a hundred armies fought at his word. Now he was a prisoner, and she, Betty, had secretly brought him a message from home.

"Who's there?" His voice was tense with hope. "Can it be you, Blondel?"

She must tell him of Blondel and the search. How worn he was! How lonely! A man caged in a tower.

"No, it's not Blondel," she was surprised to hear herself saying. "But he sends me with a message for Richard of England."

"Richard of England!" He was at the door now, his hands on the bars. "Ah, little friend, how come you in this dark tower?"

He drank in her words like a thirsty stag as she told of Blondel's accident and her own adventures in searching for him. "So you have sung throughout the land of Austria, ever waiting for a sign?"

"I promised Blondel."

"Then take this word to the Dover boat: The leopard is caged in the Tower of Gratz, but he prowls of nights in England."

He crossed the barren room to the stone wall. "But tell me more of the outside world. Are my armies yet home?"

A single window showed a star-flung sky. The candle sputtered lower in its frame, throwing monstrous shapes on the leaden walls.

"And tell me! When do you Romanys journey back again?"

"Stanko says we return with the geese when the sun moves northward."

"No—no! Go at once!" He threw out his arm in a commanding gesture. "Richard of England orders you! . . . And a man in a cage begs of you. . . ."

A dull click sounded far below. Franz had closed the tower door. She must hurry.

A quick good-bye; then she turned and, heedless of the slime of the walls, of the rounding steps, of the rats underfoot, sped like a night runner down the murky tower of Gratz.

VI

The Vision

A KNOT of gypsies stood about Stanko's camp fire. From the right came the receding clatter of a lone horseman upon the Austrian highroad.

"Will he make the Dover boat?" asked Betty.

Stanko nodded. "Boris is the swiftest rider of our tribe. No matter what happens, he will carry the word to England."

"He will make it," echoed withered Meg, the fortune teller. "He rides like the north wind across the Volga Plains." Her voice rose to a high chanting pitch. She stared before her into the leaping flames.

"Hush, little one," Stanko whispered; "Meg is one of the Chosen People of the Romanys. She visions the future in the glowing embers."

"I see a horseman gallop along the road which leads to England," Meg went on. "I see him cross the border and skirt the walls of Paris, ever spurring northward toward the Dover boat. He fumes with impatience at the wintry crossing, for he bears a message of great consequence. But the wind and tide are with him. Now is he on English soil, riding with a troubadour along the roads to London.

"I see other riders convey the tidings to all the people of the land. Rich and poor alike weep and beat their breasts, for the armies are upon the sea, and Richard is caged in Austria.

"I see the Great Council in London seated about a table. It sends heralds to every shire in

England—ransom must be sent for Richard. The lords give their taxes, the ladies their pearls and rubies. The merchants give their tapestries; the peasants give their sheep. The little children give their pennies that Richard may return to England.

"I see the great ships, returning from their long journey, sail like swans up the River Thames. At the news of their leader's imprisonment the armies rise in wrath. Their shields and armor flash in the noonday sun. As a mighty host they ride through France for Austria.

"I see Richard meet them on the way, ransomed by the jewels and gold and pennies. He sits upon a dappled charger, his sword aflame in the sunlight. Once again he leads his mighty armies, marching north to London."

Meg paused. Betty's hands were clasped in wonder at the vision. Joe was smiling at Toto, who sat at the edge of the firelit circle. A rising breeze weirdly whistled in the trees about them.

"The fire dies," Meg's voice droned on. "The vision fades. . . . Only the line of a road remains —a road with a single horseman riding through the dawn toward England."

"*The strife was long, the peril great and sore,
And heavy toil and sleepless watch he bore.
For who can turn fierce heathen from their bent
By soft persuasion and sage argument? . . .*"

THE SAXON POET

I

The Barbarian Camp

MILE after mile the road stretched through the dark forest. A canopy of drooping boughs hung over the gypsy caravan as it descended into the remote silence of the wood.

"Why is everyone behind us so quiet?" Joe whispered.

"The Romanys like not the black depths of this forest," Stanko replied. "We are on the border of the Saxon lands. Barbarians they are with deerskin clothes and long spears. They harm not the gypsies, but neither are they friendly."

Betty shivered as she peered into the dense undergrowth. "I'll be glad to see the sun again, Stanko."

"Impatience is not for the people of the road, little one. Soon we shall reach the plains of Picardy and turn southward."

"This is a good place to hunt," Joe remarked.

"Aye, wild boar with vicious tusks abound in the matted underbrush."

Silence again enveloped the forest. Only the ponies, splashing through the mud, roused now and then a sleeping beast which plunged away into a thicket. At the end of a long hard climb Stanko drew the team to a halt.

Joe touched the gypsy's sleeve. "Look—by the roadside ahead, Stanko! Two queer-looking men!"

Stanko gazed down the dusky way. "I see them not," he answered.

"They're gone now! Right into the woods they went. They had long shields and spears! Who are they, Stanko?"

The old gypsy urged forward the ponies. "Fear not, little ones. They are the Saxons—perhaps some raiding party going toward the land of their enemies, the Franks. We must get into the open country before night comes on."

Even Joe remained silent as the caravan descended the winding mountain road. Through the heavy branches he glimpsed a broad plain, shimmering like silver below them. When, hours later, they emerged from the gloom, he jumped to the ground with a shout of joy. The sound died in his throat, however, as he took in their surroundings.

Below them upon the iron-gray plain of Picardy spread the pattern of a Saxon camp. The tents of the Northern raiders dotted the level stretch for miles in each direction, with smoke curling up from a thousand barbarian fires. On the far side rose the somber walls of a castle; its towers and battlements seemed to bid high defiance to the besieging Saxon host.

"'Tis the fortified Church of St. Remy," said Stanko with widening eyes. "It is the seat of the Bishop of Reims and one of Charlemagne's favorite schools. The barbarians have laid siege to it, for in their eyes it holds much treasure. Many months will it take to make such a strong fortress open its gates to an invader."

He drew to one side to allow the other caravans to approach. "I fear it was a darkening moon that brought us this way," he went on. "Jump up, Joe; we shall turn southward and avoid this barbarian camp."

In the narrow trail ahead Joe saw a tall warrior waiting with upraised arm. The man was clothed in skins; upon his head he wore a flat leather helmet.

"Halt!"

Stanko dropped the reins. "What is it you wish? We be Romanys wandering southward toward warmer climes."

The barbarian's speech was slow and halting. "Widukind, Chief of the Saxons, demands your presence before his council fire."

"All of us?"

"Let the other wagons wait. You follow me."

He set off at a rapid stride. Stanko turned the ponies and followed him through the maze of tents. Joe was so occupied in watching these savage Northern raiders that he forgot to wonder what awaited them at the council fire of the Saxon Chief.

Outside a large goatskin tent their guide halted. "I bring them, O Chief," he cried.

Joe jumped to the ground beside Stanko. It was evident that the old gypsy was assuming for the occasion a bold mien. With a friendly smile he stepped forward to meet the lordly figure moving toward him.

"Welcome to the camp fire of Widukind, O Romanys," greeted the Chieftain.

He was garbed, Joe observed, in skins, also, and wore over his flaxen locks a gorgeous helmet of leather and beaten gold with a small cow's horn on each side. Betty remained in the van, but Joe seated himself with Stanko on the ground near the fire.

"I sent for you," began the tall Chieftain, "because I am in sore need of a messenger, an emissary, to take word to Charlemagne within the besieged Castle of St. Remy."

Stanko nodded. "Why do you not send one of your own men?"

"We have! Many times have we tried to get a message to the Frankish King, asking for his surrender; but always is our messenger shot down by an arrow from the battlements. Charlemagne fears trickery." He laughed with a wide grin that showed his pointed teeth. "We shall make them pay dearly for this!"

The Chief's cruel face had taken on an expression of malignant hatred. Joe shivered and moved closer to Stanko.

"How befalls it that the great Charlemagne is penned within the castle walls?" the gypsy inquired.

Widukind smiled as he stroked his long blond mustache. "His armies are fighting in Brittany and Aquitaine. Foolish Emperor, he remained behind in this fortified church to devote himself to the perfection of plans for schools and monasteries. Our scouts brought news of his foolishness. We came as swift as the north wind to make captive this haughty king." He proudly threw back his head; his gaze went across to the distant castle. "The walls are high and strong. For months we have battered in vain at the gate. Scouts now bring word that the Frankish armies are on the march toward St. Remy, and if we are to win we must make haste. Few men are left within the Castle. It will fall before the armies return."

"Few men remain there, say you?"

"Only women and children, and they cannot long withstand us."

"I will take the word if necessary, O Chief. Then you will allow us to continue our journey southward?"

"The Saxons never bother the gypsies who are one with the wind and the rain. But I do not wish *you* to be my messenger. You are a man; you would be shot as were my brave warriors."

"You mean——" began Stanko with a glance of surprised terror.

"Charlemagne is kind to children." The Chieftain showed his teeth again in a broad grin as he turned to Joe. "This small man shall be my messenger."

Joe felt Stanko's arm draw protectingly about

him. The old gypsy's eyes were blazing with wrath. "No!" he cried. "Not this boy! You shall not endanger him thus."

Widukind smiled cruelly. His words came like the hiss of a snake. "Disobey me in this and I shall have your gypsy tribe swept from the earth!"

Joe trembled in terror. "Let me try, Stanko," he whispered bravely. "I'll do it. I must!"

Widukind threw back his head in an evil laugh. "Yes, let him try! My messengers have never returned, and no more of my warriors shall I sacrifice. Yes, the boy shall go—go this very day!"

II

Widukind's Messenger

THE sun was low in the west when Widukind turned to Joe with the words: "Now should you make sure of your instructions. Repeat to me my message to the King of the Franks."

Joe swallowed. "My message is this: Widukind, Chief of the Saxons, demands the surrender of St. Remy. He knows that your men are few and that your armies are many weeks distant. Unless you lower the drawbridge by sunrise tomorrow, he will attack and slay without mercy."

"You have it correct. See that you repeat it so, or when you return you shall suffer."

Joe's eyes dropped before the Saxon's piercing gaze.

"Charlemagne is lost," continued the Chieftain. He pointed to the right. "Behold his departed glory!"

"I see only a plow horse at the edge of the road," observed Stanko.

Widukind laughed scornfully. "Only a plow

horse! Oh, if the great Charlemagne could hear you! It is his favorite war steed that stands before you."

Stanko stared in surprise. "What! Is that Blanco, the famous white charger of the Frankish King?"

"It is! It is! We came raiding down the mountains one early morning and sent the peasants flying. The horses of the Castle were grazing in a meadow. Charlemagne dotes on Blanco as a child on his favorite toy. And we make of him a plow horse! Every morn we plow the earth before the Castle gate so that the King may look down upon the glory that once was France."

Joe crossed to the steed that languidly stood before the wooden plow. Despite the mud that hid his glossy coat, he was a magnificent beast. He appeared neglected and untended. Yet his eyes retained their fiery challenge; they shone with a look which to Joe seemed one of unquenchable faith. No longer the beloved master bestrode his glossy back; instead, the thongs of a deadening plow enslaved him. No longer the battle cry of the Frankish King roused him to feats of valor; instead, the snap of a savage whip drove him through slimy mud.

"Poor Blanco!" Joe murmured as he patted the heaving flanks.

The horse whinnied softly. Stamping his fore-
foot in the mud he turned his head from Joe as
if ashamed that anyone who knew his name
should see him thus disgraced.

"Come, little master," Stanko called; "Widukind desires you to start at once."

Joe patted Blanco again and reluctantly

turned away. Stanko and Widukind accompanied him to the edge of the camp. Before him lay an open space, beyond which rose the Castle of St. Remy.

"Go, little master! Keep a brave heart and you will return to the caravan."

The Chieftain chuckled. "Yes, he may return —he may!"

As Joe crossed the open ground he saw that a yellow mist had descended upon the plain and that the sun was an amber ball hanging low in the west. An unnatural silence hung over the Castle; it made him think of a weird palace lying asleep for ages beneath the magic spell of a sorcerer's wand. On the high battlement he discerned a lone sentinel standing as immovable as a carven statue.

Remembering Stanko's last words of caution, Joe waved a white scarf above his head as he went forward.

"Halt!"

The sentinel had come to life; he crossed to a protruding bastion above the gate where he stood poised with drawn bow. "Who goes there?"

"A messenger!" Joe called. "A messenger from Widukind, Chief of the Saxons, to Charlemagne, King of the Franks."

"Wait!"

Three men in dull armor joined the guard. The latter disappeared. After a space of time, which seemed hours to Joe, the man reappeared.

"Come forward slowly," the guard shouted, "and the drawbridge will be lowered for you. If this means treachery, your body will be thrown from the wall."

Joe dared not glance behind. If the Saxons were planning to use this as a ruse to get the drawbridge lowered, he was in a dangerous position. At a pinch, though, he reflected, he might escape the Frankish arrows by darting back in a zigzag course. He advanced with as firm a step as he could muster, still holding the white scarf aloft.

At the moat running round the Castle wall he stopped. Suddenly he shivered as he glanced down at the black waters eddying near the banks. Opposite him the ashen wall was pierced by a great wooden gateway now closed by the uplifted bridge. A clanking of chains sounded from the gate. The drawbridge was being lowered.

With a creak of wood and a rattle of iron, the great bridge of St. Remy Castle swung slowly toward him. Joe stepped back. The drawbridge dropped with a dull thud before him. Through the dark arch of the gateway the boy could see the road to the Castle.

"Come across quickly!" a guardsman called.

Quick as a flash, Joe darted across the span. He was surrounded at once by four men in armor.

"Up with the bridge, Pierre! Hurry!"

Two men turned the great wheel; the drawbridge swung up behind him. The guardsman led him through the arched passageway into the courtyard. Joe noted that the stone building before him was unlike any castle he had yet seen. Rather was it a Gothic church with dark wine-colored windows and carven doorways. He was surprised at the quiet of the place. Except for the men who had met him and the two guardsmen on the parapet, the courtyard appeared as deserted as an ancient tomb. Where were the warriors of Charlemagne? Where were the Frankish nobles who had thus far defended the Castle from the barbarian hordes?

The Captain of the Guard beckoned to Joe. "Come this way," he ordered. "Charlemagne awaits you in the Bishop's study."

III

Charlemagne

THE guard led him to a dusky room with a vaulted roof. Three priests in black robes sat at a long table; at its head was a ruddy-faced man garbed in purple. His kindly eyes were fixed upon the messenger.

He rose as Joe advanced. The priests pushed back the bench on which they were sitting and stood also.

"Who are you?" the man in purple questioned. "You are not one of these heathen Saxons."

"No, sir," Joe answered. "I belong with Stanko's tribe of gypsies. We were passing when Widukind stopped us. He bade me come here with a message for Charlemagne."

"Speak then, lad. Charlemagne stands before you."

Joe shifted one foot. He was really in the presence of the great King of the Franks! This was Charlemagne! How his heart pounded as he spoke. "My message is this: Widukind, Chief of the Saxons, demands the immediate surrender of St. Remy——"

"Demands! Ah, the heathen!" Charlemagne's eyes flashed. "Continue. What else does he demand?"

"He says that your men are few; that your armies are weeks distant. Unless you lower the drawbridge by sunrise to-morrow he will attack and slay without mercy."

"God protect us!" murmured the priests as they sank to the bench.

Joe gazed curiously about him. The gray shadows had deepened; only a veiled light filtered through the mullioned window. Charlemagne bowed his head as he stroked his beard. "He knows our plight," Joe heard him whisper to himself. "He knows our plight."

Abruptly Charlemagne turned to the priest on his right. "Turpin," he snapped, "how many men have we left?"

"Seven able-bodied soldiers, sire."

"And the women and children?"

"Nearly four score."

"Seven men," he repeated softly, "and four-score women and children. Oh, we are lost if our armies come not to-night." He crossed to the leaden window and stared down into the court.

Turpin rose and followed. "The armies are

twelve days overdue, sire. Perhaps they will come before dawn."

Charlemagne turned. "My good Archbishop, I doubt it. But we shall fight! We shall fight to the last man!"

A stir of tapestry drew Joe's gaze to the doorway. A soldier stood there, at attention.

"What is it, Captain?" the King queried.

"A messenger, sire."

"What! Another messenger from the heathen foe?"

"No, sire. Whitewings has just returned to the East Tower."

Charlemagne looked questioningly at Archbishop Turpin. "What does he mean?"

"Whitewings is our homing pigeon, sire," returned Turpin with a note of joy and hope in his voice. "Brother Ambrose took the bird with him to Brittany. It must be a message from Count Roland."

"A message from Roland! Good news, Turpin—good news! Bring the bird at once!"

Joe drew back into the shadow of a corner. Charlemagne paced the floor in short nervous strides.

"A light, Brother Falk," the Archbishop ordered.

The priest had returned with a flaming torch

and was placing it in a niche in the wall when the servant arrived. The man carried a blue and white pigeon perched upon his arm. Joe thought he had never seen so graceful a bird as this one.

"The message, Turpin. Quick!"

"Yes, sire."

The Archbishop unstrapped a tiny packet from beneath the bird's right wing. A piece of parchment crackled as he spread it before him on the table.

"Read it, Turpin! Read it! Is it good news?"

Joe held his breath as he watched the Archbishop scan the note.

"It is from Roland, Count of the Marches of Brittany." The Archbishop coughed.

"And he says . . . ?"

The Archbishop's voice dropped lower as he answered: "The armies, sire, are four days hence."

At his words a profound silence enveloped the room. In the niche the torch flared red and gold; the leaden window was a pearl-gray square in the shadowed wall.

"Four days hence . . ." Charlemagne's voice dropped to a whisper. His hands fell to his knees in a gesture of despair. "We are lost, Turpin! We are lost!"

The Captain of the Guard stepped forward.

With bitter hatred and fury in his eyes he pointed to Joe. "This messenger, sire—shall we not throw his body back to the heathen?"

Joe's face went white. He threw a beseeching glance toward Charlemagne. Was this to be his end? Had Widukind been right? . . . Would he never again see Betty and Stanko and the green van?

Charlemagne raised his hand. "Let the messenger be, Captain. We shall have no useless murders upon our hands." His voice dropped to a sigh. "It matters not—one small boy will neither lose nor save the Castle."

The Captain bowed low. "Shall I put him in the dungeon, sire?"

"Let him be," returned Charlemagne. "He shall take his chances with the rest. Why hurry his end—when to-morrow morning the Castle walls will fall. . . ."

The Armor Room

JOE sat on the rear bench in the Bishop's chapel. As it was candle-lighting time, the people of the Castle were at vespers. Joe had been put into the hands of one of the guardsmen, and that man now silently sat next to him, his eyes intent upon the priest at the altar. A melancholy quiet brooded over the company. Tall white candles gleamed softly; the organ's haunting sadness merged into the steady beat of rain at the windows.

At the last forlorn note the guardsman, with a quick glance at Joe, slipped from the chapel. Outside the door he paused.

"Perhaps to-morrow night," he said, "some heathen god will be worshiped here. Come, you are to sup with me in the refectory. This is a short way there."

Joe followed him into a long gloomy room where armor was piled row on row against the wall. About him lay helmets, coats of mail, shields, and spears, all in neat rows and rising to a height far above his head.

"What room is this?" Joe asked.

"Oh, this is the armory. Over there are the helmets and coats of mail that once were worn by our brave knights who fell in the last two on-slaughts. Over here is the new armor that the craftsmen have prepared for the returning ar-mies."

"There must be hundreds of suits of mail here."

"Near to a thousand. Were they filled with men, Widukind and his heathen hordes would never take this Castle."

Joe intently gazed about. "Yes, if they were only filled with men," he mused. "I heard Widu-kind say he would not dare another attack if he knew the Castle was well garrisoned."

At supper Joe hardly noticed the storm that raged outside like some great beast unloosed by the Saxon storm god; the wind bellowed about the towers and battlements; the rain beat and pounded at the shuttered windows. He was ab-sorbed by his thoughts. When the meal neared its end he spoke to the guardsman:

"Do you think Charlemagne would let me speak with him?"

The man stared in amazement. "Truly you are a forward lad. No; but you might speak with the Archbishop. Brother Falk, this lad would have learnèd converse with the Archbishop."

The guardsman chuckled at his joke; yet the priest rose and strode across to the table on the dais where Charlemagne and the ladies were seated with the Archbishop. Trembling with apprehension, Joe watched Brother Falk bend over to whisper his message into the ear of the prelate.

A moment later the priest returned with the words: "The Archbishop will see you now."

Joe was thankful that the assembled people, evidently lost in their own dark forebodings, did not notice him as he climbed the few steps to the higher table.

"Speak, lad," said the churchman kindly. "What is it?"

With the beating of his heart loud in his ears, the boy vaguely murmured, "Widukind—you think he will attack in the morning?"

"At sunrise—alas!"

"What's this you're saying?" broke in Charlemagne.

"I heard Widukind talking," said Joe in a more confident tone. "He said that if he thought the Castle still had many fighters, he would not dare another attack. He knows that your armies are hurrying to your assistance."

"He knows our men are few? God grant, not how few!"

"He isn't sure," Joe continued, gaining courage. "If he were to see a thousand men upon the battlements, he would flee before the return of your warriors."

Charlemagne smiled grimly. "A thousand men? We have seven."

"'Tis hopeless, lad," said the Archbishop. "We can only pray."

Joe stood his ground. "But if Widukind *thought* you had a thousand men . . ."

He paused to examine the faces of his listeners. They were utterly quiet now; all were gazing at him in wonder.

"If Widukind thought!" echoed Charlemagne. "What do you mean?"

The words fairly rushed from Joe's lips. "The guard took me through the armor room. There I saw hundreds of suits of mail—hundreds of helmets!"

"Yes, and all useless, useless! Would that they were filled with men!"

"That's it," cried Joe. "Fill them!"

"Fill them?"

"Yes, with anything! With priests, with women, with children, with wood! Stand them against the battlements! When the sun comes up its rays will strike against burnished steel; the Saxons will think a thousand fighters are waiting for the attack."

A gasp of sheer surprise went round the table. Charlemagne looked at Turpin. Understanding gleamed in the eyes of both.

The Archbishop smote the table an unaccustomed blow. "Sire, 'tis possible! Willingly would I crack a heathen pate before I die!"

"A thousand suits of mail!" murmured the Frankish King. "A thousand knights in armor flashing on the parapet at rise of sun! 'Tis possible, Turpin. There is one chance in a hundred, but we shall grasp it. Egad! This lad of ours has wits!"

He rose to a commanding height. "Call the Captain of the Guard!" he cried. "Call the carpenter! Call the women of the Castle! We shall work this night as we have never worked before. Please God, the Castle shall not fall!"

V

On the Battlements

ALL night long the storm furiously lashed the Castle. All night long the people toiled unceasingly. Torches flared like molten gold upon the ramparts; women climbed the long flights of stairs from the cellar with huge black logs on their shoulders; carpenters sawed and hacked at the wood, while others clothed the wooden soldiers in gorgeous suits of mail.

Joe paused a moment in his labor to peer over the parapet. The continual downpour had blotted out even the Saxon fires; a rushing sea of wind and rain surged below the Castle walls. If the barbarian hordes were preparing for the attack at dawn, their movements were shrouded in a heavy pall of blackness.

The boy wondered if the Saxon guards had noted the unusual flare of torches on the battlements. The flames hissed like a nest of vipers as they coiled and writhed against the wet wall.

Joe's thoughts were interrupted by the voice

of a guardsman near by. "Where's a log?" the man called.

"Here!" he cried in answer. "Here's a big one."

He dragged a huge timber to the workman.

"We need a wooden knight six feet tall to fill this suit of mail," went on the guardsman. "Here, little gypsy, help me dress this cavalier."

He chuckled dryly. Joe held the log upright while the guardsman slipped over it the coat of mail. "Now for the helmet!" The man closed the visor and set the shining steel headpiece upon the sagging shoulders.

"Aye, a stalwart warrior. Surely even a hundred such should strike terror to heathen hearts."

Together they lifted the dummy to the bastion and propped it against the parapet. The battlement was already lined with a hundred immobile figures, all standing in dignified silence as though poised for the attack. The dancing torchlight playing on the glistening steel of their armor was reflected in pools of rain water at their feet.

Just before dawn the downpour slackened. By the time the saffron glow in the east had deepened to the color of burnt orange, Joe discovered that their task was finished. He had donned with the rest a helmet with upflung visor and a coat of mail that hung in ripples about his knees.

"Keep moving! Keep moving!" The order circled the wall.

Joe paraded back and forth on the bastion above the great gate of the Castle. A ray of sunlight tinged the driving clouds with rose and gold. The gray plain took on form and color. Intently Joe watched the rising mist. Before his astonished eyes the meadow stirred and quickened to action. He gasped in dismay. The Saxon army was marching toward them.

At a muttered exclamation, Joe turned. A few feet away stood Charlemagne. He was in earnest conversation with another mail-clad figure which Joe recognized as that of His Reverence, the Archbishop of Reims.

"They come, Turpin! They come!" Charlemagne drew his sword and flashed it in the sun.

"But they haven't seen us yet, sire. Wait! . . ."

Joe glanced at the meadow below. The last bit of rain and mist had disappeared, and now the early sunlight shot into every corner of the plain. Slowly and steadily the barbarian hordes advanced. Their relentless approach was like some great incoming tidal wave which would break about the walls and engulf the fortress in a hissing, foaming torrent.

At the head of the army rode Widukind upon his coal-black charger. Clearly now Joe saw his

"Come here, my lad," said Charlemagne

helmet with the cow horns pointing skyward.
The Chief was rallying his warriors for the final
attack; soon the priceless treasures of the Castle
would be in their hands. The foremost barbarians
carried logs and branches. Behind them two
dozen men labored under the weight of a great
battering ram made from a huge tree trunk
which their oxen had hauled from the mountains. When a pathway of the branches had been
made across the moat, the battering ram would
pound at the gate of St. Remy.

As the last cloud was driven across the sky,
the sun blazed forth in all its early splendor,
splashing the Castle with tints of gold and saffron.
Joe saw the Saxons halt, puzzled. A stifled cry
of amazement went up from the ranks.

Thousands of mail-clad warriors lined the ramparts of what they had thought an almost deserted Castle. Wonderment gave way to terror.
This was magic! This was witchery! The Castle
had been bereft of all fighting men, and here in
the morning light shone the helmets of a thousand warriors.

Magic! Black Magic! Men they could fight,
but not demons. Run—run! Flee from this sudden terror.

Joe watched with rising hope. The barbarians
swung round in confusion. In horror and dismay

they fled from the field. In a moment of joyful exultation Joe reflected that they were like so many rats fleeing from the sight of a stuffed cat gazing placidly down upon them.

Almost in a flash oxen were harnessed to the crude wooden wagons. Tents were pulled down with great speed by the terror-stricken mob. Leaving half their belongings behind them, they made straight for the mountains.

"They have gone, Turpin!" Charlemagne leaned on the parapet. "I cannot believe my eyes. Look and tell me if you see the same—are they fleeing?"

"Like so many scared rabbits, sire."

Cheers circled the Castle walls. Running clumsily in their unaccustomed suits, the women hurried along the ramparts to the bastion. In the midst of this scene stood Charlemagne. Suddenly he wheeled. His eyes went round the throng till they came to the spot where Joe stood against the parapet.

"Come here, my lad," said Charlemagne.

Joe dragged at his helmet. Beneath the eager gaze of the onlookers he timidly advanced.

"Kneel!"

The little circle crowded closer. Joe dropped to his knees before the Frankish King. His cheeks flushed. What did this mean?

Charlemagne smiled down at him. "Truly you have saved us, O Little Friend of the Franks. Never shall we forget this day."

He raised his sword and gently touched Joe's shoulder. "I hereby dub you knight. Arise, Sir Joseph, Knight of St. Remy!"

VI

Blanco

THE great drawbridge of St. Remy was lowered. In high glee the people of the Castle trooped across the moat. They rejoiced, Joe reflected, as though a sorcerer's spell had been lifted from their Castle.

"Free! Free!" they shouted. "Free once more."

They frolicked about on the turf like holiday children. Charlemagne, whose tall form towered above the heads of his people, stood looking out across the meadow toward the mountains into which the Saxons had disappeared. He was searching for something there.

"I see your gypsies coming," he remarked to Joe.

"Stanko? Where? Where?"

Joe ran ahead to get clear of the merrymakers. He saw, creeping toward them across the plain, the green van, a mere toy upon the vast level. Though he knew Stanko and Betty could not possibly see him, he waved his hand.

He turned to look back at Charlemagne. The King's gaze was still searching the horizon. Suddenly Joe saw his face light up with surprise and joy. Coming swiftly toward them through the litter of the barbarian camp was a lone horse. A wooden thing dragged at the animal's heels.

"Blanco!" Charlemagne cried as he hurried forward. "He has escaped from the heathen!"

Like a rush of wind the great white charger of the Frankish King came tearing across the space, whinnying at every step. The circle about the King pushed back as the horse approached. Without an instant's hesitation he trotted up to Charlemagne. He stopped before his master, reared upon his hind legs, and neighed eagerly.

"Aye, Blanco," whispered Charlemagne. Quick as a flash, he sprang to the horse's back; he stroked the muddy shoulders and the proudly arched neck.

Hands tore at the leather thongs. The wooden plow was thrown aside. The animal seemed to sense freedom again; once more he was carrying his beloved master. He stamped the ground as if impatient to be off on the march to battle.

At the touch of Charlemagne's boot on the horse's flank, the charger swung off in a great circle across the meadow.

As a rumble of wheels on the baked earth

reached his ears, Joe roused himself. Mimo and Zulieka were drawing the green van closer as fast as their little hoofs could travel.

The boy ran forward. "Stanko!" he called. "Stanko!" His heart swelled with joy as he beheld Betty jumping up and down on the seat and waving her gypsy kerchief. Only for an instant did he pause to look back at the Castle lying shrouded in the golden haze of the morning.

"'*O King of the Faithful,*' *said Sheherazade,*
'*if that strange story has beguiled thy waking*
hours, listen then to this . . .'"

ARABIAN NIGHTS

I

The Road to Bagdad

AHEAD of us, little ones, lies Bagdad."
Stanko threw out his hand, pointing across the vast expanse of desert. Betty and Joe looked toward the eastern horizon, where against the Arabian sky rose the dim outlines of a magic city of glittering domes and minarets.

"It's still far off," Betty murmured.

Stanko nodded. "Half a day's journey. It is called the City of a Thousand Wonders. There lives the good Caliph Haroun al Rashid."

"Boris says the Arabs worship him," broke in Joe.

"And well they may. 'Tis said that the Caliph

tramps the streets and lanes by night, disguised as a seller of rugs or perhaps a goatherd, to see if his officers govern the city as he wishes. He would have even the lowliest of his subjects contented." Stanko urged on the ponies. "Glad shall we be to reach the gorgeous bazaars of Bagdad, for there shall we buy rugs and silks to peddle at the great country fairs in the North."

At that moment Betty clutched his arm. "What's that by the roadside?"

"Only a donkey grazing."

"To the right of the donkey, I mean."

Stanko stared. "Strange doings are these! It appears to be a man fettered with thongs!"

Stanko halted the ponies and jumped to the ground. Betty and Joe followed. A strange sight met their eyes.

Near the donkey, which unconcernedly grazed by the roadside, was the prone form of a man, doubtless the owner, writhing in an effort to free himself from the heavy cords that bound his hands and feet.

"What does this mean?" cried Stanko as he knelt to slash the fetters with his knife.

The stranger, a bronzed Arab in flowing blue robes, sat up with a wry smile. "Robbers!" he returned in a cool even voice. "Desert thieves overtook me and stole all I had. I am a poor camel driver of Bagdad. Look, all that is left of my worldly wealth is one donkey."

He pointed toward the small beast that blinked at them lazily for a moment before turning to graze again on the sparse grass and camel thorn.

"Robbers!" Joe repeated.

The Arab nodded. "By the Prophet, I shall punish them for this outrage! The Caliph of Bagdad—may Allah give him years unnumbered! —has cleared the city of thieves and beggars, but the desert highways are still menaced by a robber band. Forty strong, they gallop over the sands on their *meharis*—riding camels of the fastest breed. The Caliph has searched in vain for their hiding place. Always do they escape."

"Always?" Betty murmured.

"Allah has allowed them to escape once more. But wait!" The camel driver raised his head proudly; his dark eyes flashed.

Stanko motioned him toward the van. "We Romanys go to the bazaars to buy rugs and silks. Will you ride with us?"

"May the Prophet reward your courtesy, O Gypsy." The Arab rose. "Gladly will I accept. . . . Perhaps the boy would drive my donkey with the ponies of your caravan."

Betty gazed with longing at the small beast

with drooping ears. "Oh, let me ride him," she begged; "I'm tired of the van."

Stanko looked undetermined. The camel driver threw back his head and laughed. "She is safe upon Salam. Never has he been known to go faster than a walk."

At Stanko's nod of assent Joe enviously helped Betty to the back of the surprised donkey. The Arab twisted a rope about the beast's nose and gave the end to Betty. "Use this for a switch," he counseled; "you will have need of it if you would keep abreast of the van. Go, Salam. Go!"

Salam slowly turned his head and blinked.

"Go on, Salam!" cried Betty.

Salam returned with indifference to his meal of camel thorn.

Joe grinned, and even Stanko smiled. That was enough for Betty; she struck the donkey two unexpected blows with the rope.

Salam gave her a surprised, offended glance, then he moved in a slow, measured tread along the highroad.

"We're off!" called Betty joyfully.

Stanko flicked the reins. "Do not drop behind the caravan, little one," he cautioned. "The road is lonely and dangerous."

Although Betty urged her mount to his swiftest, the donkey lagged behind. Van after van

overtook her. Boris called a greeting; Meg proph-
esied that she would never reach Bagdad upon
that swift steed. Betty only laughed. It was fun,
even if Salam did require upon her part a greater
outlay of energy than she would need in walking.

Soon she was hopelessly behind the gypsies.
The last van was far ahead, almost hidden by the
yellow dust of the road. "Oh, I wish I hadn't
ridden this old donkey," she sighed as she gave
Salam another whack. "I can't leave him here
or the poor camel driver will lose his last animal."

At that moment Salam stopped. His ears shot
up and he gazed to the left across the rocky
desert. Betty, looking in that direction, saw three
donkeys in a sea of dust coming toward her.
Upon the first was seated a hooded Arab.

"On, Salam! On!" she urged. "We don't want
to meet any strangers upon this lonely road."

Salam, however, thought otherwise. He evidently wanted companionship of his own kind.
Betty's pleadings were in vain; the whack of the
rope's end merely made him blink. He had decided to stop, and nothing would move him.

With grave misgivings, Betty watched the
approach of the strange Arab.

II

Ali Baba

AS HE drew near, the Arab threw back his hood and smiled reassuringly. "Greetings, O Stranger," he said. "Glad am I to have company on the road to Bagdad, for a most unusual sight have I seen this morning."

Betty's fear vanished; in its place came curiosity. "An unusual sight! What was it?"

"I am a woodcutter," the man went on; "and a moment ago as I was cutting wood in yonder dry river bed, I saw a small caravan of forty horses and camels coming toward me."

"Forty horses and camels!"

"Thieves, I think their riders were; else why should they travel so secretly along the dry course of a river?"

Betty's eyes widened. "Can it be the Forty Thieves that the Caliph of Bagdad wishes to capture? They attacked a poor camel driver near here this morning."

"Perhaps it was the same robber band. But

how should I know! I am only Ali Baba, a wood-cutter of the city."

"Why didn't you watch?" cried Betty, exasperated at this simple fellow. "They may have a hiding place near by."

Ali Baba remained silent a moment. "I did not wish to be seen watching."

Betty gazed across the yellow plain to a thin line of trees that marked the course of the river. Gone now were her fears, and Stanko's counsel she only vaguely remembered. Adventures had become her daily food, and here was another dish to be served at her bidding. It was an opportunity also to help the poor Arab they had picked up on the road that morning. What could a man do, she reflected, with only one donkey like Salam? Doubtless the thieves had not thought such a lazy animal worth owning. If she and Ali Baba could only find this hiding place!

"Come," she cried with sudden decision, "we will go to the edge of the river and hide behind the rocks. We may see where the robbers go."

The woodcutter eyed her in amazement. "'Tis dangerous! What would happen if we were seen?"

Betty tossed aside his arguments. "We shall only watch," she urged. "Come, you may gain favor with the Caliph."

She started across the sandy waste. Ali Baba glanced at her uncertainly, then, leaving the two rear donkeys to graze, he reluctantly followed.

They left the road behind and took to the open plain; they passed around great bowlders that blocked their way, ever making toward the distant line of trees that bordered the river bed. These they approached with caution. Ali Baba dismounted and tied his beast to a branch of low tamarisk. Betty, following his example, led the way up the river bank.

"Caution, little friend," Ali Baba whispered. "It was toward this spot that the caravan was moving."

Near the top of the slope Ali Baba with infinite care climbed a white mulberry tree, the leafy branches of which securely hid him from the eyes of anyone passing in the river road below. Betty peered from behind a great bowlder. She caught her breath in sharp surprise.

Silently following the dry course of the river marched the caravan that Ali Baba had seen. Leading the way were half a dozen armed guards mounted on quivering dark horses. After them came the line of camels. The ungainly desert beasts were loaded with great bales of goods— loot, probably, ravished from travelers bound to the coast from Samarkand or Teheran. On each side walked robed men carrying long spears and knives. Yes, without doubt there must be forty men at least!

Ali Baba whispered down to her: "A rough-looking lot. Thieves without doubt."

Betty nodded. A warm breeze wandered along the gorge; the mulberry rustled mysteriously, and the dwarf tamarisk shrubs whined dismally near her. Abruptly she drew back. The leader of the hooded Arabs had stopped the caravan. He dismounted from his horse and came toward the river bank. Betty trembled. Had he seen her? Glancing up at Ali Baba, she saw that he had flattened himself upon a branch of the tree. His face had turned a sickly white.

Below her she heard the Arab's approaching footsteps; the crunch of his slippered feet on the pebbles suddenly stopped, and the deep guttural tones of his voice floated up to her.

"Open, Sesame!"* he commanded. "Open, Sesame!"

Again Betty peered from her hiding place. She almost gasped in amazement, for directly below them stood the hawklike Captain of the Thieves, garbed in flowing robes of crimson. His beady black eyes searched the rocks of the slope. "Open, Sesame!" he repeated.

*Pronounced Ses-sem-my.

Betty stared. With a crunching sound a huge rock slowly moved to one side. Visible in the burning sunlight was the dark opening of a cave. The leader motioned to his men, then disappeared into the dark interior. Immediately the thirty-nine thieves followed him with the bales of loot upon their shoulders. Betty dared hardly breathe as she watched the camels being unloaded and the goods transported into the hiding place.

Presently they came out again and mounted their beasts. The leader paused at the entrance. Betty heard his voice raised in command: "Close, Sesame!"

The huge bowlder rolled across the entrance. The Captain turned and mounted his restless thoroughbred; then the caravan swung about and quietly passed along the ravine.

Ali Baba slid down the tree trunk. " 'Tis their hiding place. Would that I could load one of my donkeys with their gold——"

"If we could only get into the cave!" broke in Betty. "We would lead the Caliph's men to the stolen goods."

Ali Baba sighed. "We could tell them, but to go to the cave would be too dangerous. No, we wouldn't dare. . . ."

Betty surveyed the rocks before the entrance.

"Do you think, Ali Baba, that the rock would move if we stood at the entrance and cried: 'Open, Sesame'?"

The woodcutter shook his head. "No—no! It is too dangerous. . . . It looks like magic—black magic! I will have nothing to do with it."

"But if you gained favor with the Caliph, Ali Baba! If we could lead his men to this very cave and open the way for them, what would not be yours for the asking? Think, Ali Baba! Let us learn the secret of the cave. I'll watch here while you go down the bank and give the sign."

Ali Baba looked at her in terror. "I? Never! I am merely a poor woodcutter of Bagdad. I am only Ali Baba. How could I——"

Scorn was in Betty's voice. "Then you will probably always remain a poor woodcutter, Ali Baba. Look, I am not afraid." She started down the slope.

"Where are you going?" wailed Ali Baba.

"I am going to the cave," she answered.

Ali Baba threw out his arms toward Mecca. "May Allah protect us," he moaned. "May a thousand plagues descend upon the Forty Thieves. May the river open and swallow their horses and camels."

With a trembling step he trailed after Betty.

III

The Secret Cave

AT THE huge rock which blocked the entrance to the secret cave the woodcutter joined her. "I am not afraid," he said, with chattering teeth. "No, I am not afraid."

Betty smiled. "Say the words now, Ali Baba," she urged. "If there is danger, we can run."

Ali Baba nodded. His hands fumbled at his throat as if he would make it obey his wishes. When he spoke, his voice was almost a groan. "Open, Sesame. . . . Open, Sesame."

"Louder! Louder!"

"Open, Sesame!" Ali Baba's voice quavered with fear. He suddenly started and turned as if to run. Betty held him back with a detaining hand.

The great rock before the entrance was slowly swinging aside. Opening before them was a dark passageway which curved to the left into utter darkness.

"Look!" Ali Baba cried. He pointed to the rock above the entrance.

Betty, raising her eyes, saw graven on the rock a small design: a crescent moon and dagger. "What is it?" she asked.

Ali Baba's eyes rolled wildly. "It is the mark of the Forty Thieves," he stuttered. "Always do they place it on their stolen goods." He looked warily round and his voice sank to a whisper. "Sometimes a dealer in the Market Place will find that mark upon his favorite camel or upon some rare rug from Kairwan. And always does the marked goods disappear! No one knows how! It goes——" Ali Baba waved his arms as if he would show how magic was used to spirit away the coveted article to the coffers of the Forty Thieves.

"Come," urged Betty, "we will enter the cave together."

She led the way slowly into the dark passage. Ali Baba followed at her heels. Far down the tunnel they soon saw a glimmer of light, and toward this Betty now began to hurry. As they advanced she noticed a musty odor rushing out

to meet them. It enveloped them in cold air like
a breeze off wintry peaks. Abruptly the passageway widened into an immense underground
chamber. On the threshold Betty looked about
with eyes aglow.

The stronghold of the robbers was a chamber,
circular in form; it was lighted from an opening
far above, through which entered the faint rays
of the sun. On the walls were rare tapestries and
rugs; embroideries of Oriental design were flung
over chests and bales. Dull wine-colored brocades
gleamed in the mellow light.

"It is beautiful!" murmured Betty. "See the
colors! Gold and purple."

Ali Baba breathed excitedly at her elbow.
"Here lies the wealth of the world, little friend.
One bag would make me the wealthiest man in
our street."

He hurried forward to a half-open bag and dug
his hands into the dull yellow coins. "Gold!" he
whispered. "Gold pilfered from caravans returning from Mecca." He filled the pockets beneath
his flowing robe. "The robbers will never miss
a few pieces; yet will this gold set my family
well on the way to comfort."

Betty meanwhile surveyed the innumerable
treasures. She noted on each chest and on each
bale of silk the small mark of the Forty Thieves.

With a shudder she turned away from that crescent moon and dagger. A strange aromatic perfume struck her nostrils, and looking closely, she
saw in one corner an incense brazier with a blue
coil of smoke ascending toward the light. The air
was scented with the aromatic fragrance of the
East: jasmine and lilac, geranium and attar of
rose.

"Hist!" Ali Baba suddenly whispered.

Betty whirled. The woodcutter raised his hand
in warning.

"Something's coming—down the ravine. Do
you hear?"

Betty listened. She heard far in the distance
the rhythmic sound of hoof beats on the rocks
of the river bed.

She grasped Ali Baba's trembling hand.
"Come—we must go."

Swiftly they ran down the passageway. At the
entrance they paused. Peering down the ravine,
they made out the figure of a solitary rider coming toward them.

"We must run," Betty whispered.

Without a word Ali Baba ran into the open
and raced up the slope toward his mount.

Outside the entrance Betty stopped short.
"Close, Sesame!" she cried. Even as she turned
to flee, she heard a crunching noise as the rock

slid into place again. Quickly she ran up the rocky bank.

Ali Baba had already mounted his donkey. "Hurry, little friend," he urged. "We must ride for the city. There shall we be safe, once we are lost in the crowds of the bazaars."

Salam blinked lazily at Betty when she jumped to his back; but a few taps with her rope sent him hurrying down the slope and across the plain.

"Think you it was one of the thieves returning?" Ali Baba alighted from his unsteady beast.

Betty nodded.

"Then will he follow us," the woodcutter wailed. "These thieves will never allow us to get away with the loot; they will creep after us and mark my house." His voice rose to a high mournful pitch. "Oh, woe to me and my family! We shall all be killed!"

Betty glanced back. Instantly her face went white. Standing on the ridge and clearly outlined against the yellow sky was the figure of a robed horseman.

IV

The City of a Thousand Wonders

JUST outside the great North Gate of Bagdad, in the shadow of the towered wall, a caravansary greets the traveler from across the desert wastes. Here in the noisy courtyard Ali Baba left their donkeys. He and Betty took to their heels, hoping thus to escape the eyes of any follower of the robber chief.

They entered the city by the Gate of the Talisman, and at once the great heart of Bagdad enfolded them. As they made their way through the crowded streets Betty grasped Ali Baba's hand. About them swarmed the slow-moving Arabs dressed in flowing robes. Above the shuffle of slippered feet on the dust of the alleys sounded the strange nasal cries of the East. Occasionally a camel driver stopped to gaze curiously at Betty hurrying along at Ali Baba's side.

"Are we followed, little one?" Ali Baba asked.

Betty glanced over her shoulder. "I cannot tell, Ali Baba; all these strange people in their

robes look alike to me. And their eyes! How black they are—and how glittering!"

"This way." The woodcutter turned down a shaded lane that curved between two blank walls.

Presently they emerged into the crowded

Market Place. Here were gathered people from all the East: merchants with dates, coffee, and perfumes; rug sellers from Kairwan; pilgrims from Samarkand; ivory dealers from across the deserts of Africa. A passing beggar with drooping head lifted a supplicating hand. "A coin, O Wealthy One," he whined; "in the name of Allah, the Merciful, the Compassionate——"

Ali Baba gave the fakir a disdainful glance. "May Allah satisfy all your wants, O Brother to a Camel."

Betty saw the beggar flinch at the insult. With pity she noted his tattered garments and stooping figure. "Give him a coin," she urged. "See how old he is, how hungry——" She paused and looked more closely at the man. Something about him was vaguely familiar. In spite of the whine, she had heard this voice before. Now she remembered; he reminded her of the poor camel driver they had found by the roadside that morning, the man who had told them about the quest of the Caliph for the Forty Thieves. She knitted her brows as she gazed searchingly at the beggar, but his face was turned away.

Ali Baba reached into the voluminous folds of his robe and dropped a glittering gold piece into the dust. Instantly the beggar was down on his knees like some small animal seeking food.

He rose with smiling face. "May Allah bless you a thousand times," he crooned.

Ali Baba shook his head in despair. "'Twas not wisely done, little friend from the North. See where he has gone—straight to the coffee shop of Hadji Ahmed. He might have chosen a stall where food is cheap in the Street of the Milk Sellers' Market."

From the minaret of a near-by mosque the prayer call of the muezzin fell on the evening air. Prayer rugs were brought forth, and the Mohammedans dropped to the ground, faces toward Mecca. Ali Baba reverently joined the throng of worshipers repeating in soft tones: "There is only one God, and Mohammed is His Prophet."

Athrob with interest Betty quietly watched. There was a final murmur and the prayer was finished. Chatter broke out as the Moslems folded their rugs and turned toward home.

Ali Baba again took Betty's hand, and swiftly they crossed the Market Place. Evening was near. Already purple shadows were gathering across the arcaded square; candles were being lighted behind grated windows. When they turned into the covered Street of the Tent Makers' Bazaar, Ali Baba, with a frightened glance backward, quickened his pace. Above the shuffle of passing footsteps, the tinkle of goats' bells, and the murmur of Arab voices rose the unmistakable sound of an approaching horseman.

"The spy!" Ali Baba choked. "He follows!"

Betty glanced back. Coming swiftly after them was the mounted form of a lone rider. She at once recognized him as the robber sentinel.

"We must hide, Ali Baba." Her voice was commanding. She pulled her companion into a side alley that twisted away into the deepening twilight. Pressing themselves flat against the wall, they waited.

"'Tis he!" Ali Babi whispered. "We are doomed."

The beat of approaching hoofs grew louder. Even as they waited, darkness descended. The flame left the western sky; the purple shadows turned to deepest indigo; somewhere in a hidden garden behind them the night breeze began to sing in the fig trees. The horseman went by, unseeing. His hooded figure was like some ghost riding through the dusk. The sound of the horse's hoofs abruptly stopped.

Ali Baba clutched Betty's arm. "He is dismounting! He knows we have taken to a side alley. Come!"

They plunged down the twisting lane. Behind jalousied windows lamps gleamed pure gold; above shone the blue-green of the luminous desert night. A cloaked figure scuffled softly past, while from over the housetops came the throb of a native tom-tom beating rhythmically its wild, strange dance. Night had descended upon the oasis city of Bagdad.

When the crescent moon came stealing into the shadowy Street of the Tent Makers' Bazaar the two fugitives crept back to the Market Place and quietly crossed to a second side street. Here the narrow twisting alleys engulfed them. Betty felt lost in the dark maze of blank walls and curving lanes. Once they stopped, for Betty thought she heard slippered feet creeping after them. But it must have been the pounding of her heart, for the street remained silent. Whispering voices from above made her glance upward. Women with veiled faces leaned over the parapets of the mud-walled houses to gaze down at them.

"We are near the house of my family," Ali Baba whispered.

Betty was not sorry. She was almost exhausted from their flight. When her companion reached a doorway and knocked softly once, twice, she wondered how he could possibly know his own house in this street where all doors looked exactly alike. She leaned for a moment against the wall. Her eyes, roaming over the scene through which they had passed, suddenly widened with fear.

Along the shadowed wall slipped the white-robed form of an Arab.

In a flash she grasped Ali Baba's hand. "Look!" she breathed. "We are followed."

Even as she spoke, she saw their pursuer flatten himself against the wall and his figure imperceptibly merge into the darkness.

V

The Marked House

THE welcoming cries of Ali Baba's wife and brood of children were like sweet music to Betty's ears. Marjanieh, a girl of Betty's age, was sent to the roof to watch the street while the family sat down to a supper of cous-cous and goat's milk served on the floor. After the meal, when Marjanieh had returned with the news that the street remained deserted, Ali Baba's spirits rose.

"We have outwitted them," he chuckled. "The thieves do not know by which door we entered. Now shall we have sugared figs and spices upon our table. Ah, 'tis a good world!"

Ali Baba's wife smiled. "You feel as does that new poet who has taken the city by storm. He is a tent maker who once lived near by—Omar by name."

"He makes better verse," Ali Baba remarked, "than he does tents."

His wife turned upon him with scorn in her voice. "And you, Ali Baba, make neither tents nor verse. . . . Repeat his newest rhyme, Marjanieh. How goes it?"

Betty eagerly listened while Marjanieh proudly repeated her lines:

"Ah, fill the Cup: What boots it to repeat
How Time is slipping underneath our Feet:
Unborn To-morrow, dead Yesterday,
Why fret about them if To-day be sweet!——"

Marjanieh abruptly stopped. A slight scraping at the door struck her into silence. Ali Baba stifled the cries of his youngest child, while his wife and Betty tiptoed to the door. There, athrob with excitement, they listened.

Unmistakably, they heard the soft shuffle of sandaled feet fading into the distant sounds of the bazaars.

"We shall all be killed," wailed Ali Baba. "Yes, even to my youngest man-child——"

"Be silent, O Fool of a Donkey Driver," hissed his wife. "It may be only a pariah dog scratching at the door for food."

She turned to Betty. "Get a candle, little friend, and we shall open the door."

Together they unlatched the wooden door. Betty held high the candle while they gazed into the street. Far down the moonlit way they made out a cloaked figure disappearing round a corner.

"Look!" cried Ali's wife, pointing to the door.

Betty stared. High on the dark wood was the chalk mark of a crescent moon and dagger—the mark of the Forty Thieves. . . .

Ali Baba, his face as white as the mark on the door, struggled to his feet. "The mark of the Forty Thieves! We are lost—lost!"

His wife closed the door with a bang. "Hush your tongue, O Husband of Little Courage. 'Tis easily perceived whence comes the efficiency of our youngest child at crying in the night."

She turned to Betty. "We shall get water and wash the mark from the door."

One of the children brought hot water from the kitchen, and they set to work. Ali's wife scrubbed first, but the mark refused to disappear. Betty tried next without better effect. "The chalk has dug deep into the wood," she remarked. "Even if we do wash away the chalk, the mark will still be there in the morning."

Ali Baba's wife nodded. "If we cannot get this

mark from the door, then we are indeed lost. We shall have to flee before sunrise."

Betty thoughtfully surveyed the street. "All the houses are exactly alike," she mused. "If every door in this street were marked like this, no one would be able to pick your house from the lot."

"Mark them all!" cried Ali's wife. "Truly it is the very thing! Marjanieh, bring our little friend a piece of chalk from your school box." She turned to Betty, yet raised her voice so Ali Baba would hear. "Truly you are worth ten men, little friend."

Presently Betty, chalk in hand, slipped into the moonlit street. Ali Baba's wife closed the door after her. Betty glanced up and down the shadowy way, but only the blank walls of the houses met her eyes. The silence of the street was profound; only now and then some night bird fluttered over the roofs on its way to the river.

She crept to the first door to the right and outlined upon it a crescent moon and dagger.

Her hand was firm and her stroke deft, for the mark upon the bales and chests in the cave had been graven upon her memory. At the third door she paused. A nervous tread within the house assailed her ears like the sudden throb of a war drum. She slipped to one side and pressed her body against the wall. Her heart pounded in terror. But the sound was not repeated, and she passed on to the next house.

From door to door she slipped; when she returned once more, the houses up and down the street all bore the emblem of the Forty Thieves.

As she went in, she traced again the sign upon their own door.

Ali Baba's wife sighed in relief. "Now the robbers will have a merry time finding this house."

"Do you think," broke in Ali Baba, "that it would be better if I left the city for a few days? I might go to my brother's——"

"Be still, O Brother of a Donkey," his wife shrilled. "You and our little friend must remain hidden within these walls. To-morrow morning a dozen men from the robber band will be searching this street for the dwelling with the brand of the Forty Thieves upon it."

VI

The Caliph of Bagdad

ALL next morning Betty and Ali Baba remained in the darkened room. The children reported that several strange men were patroling the street. Betty was sure they were the followers of the robber chief vainly searching for the house which one of them had marked the night before.

"If we could only get word to the Caliph," Betty remarked, "then the guards might capture the robbers. We might send Marjanieh to the palace."

"Oh, but I wouldn't dare ask for the Caliph," Marjanieh remonstrated.

At that moment one of the children came running with the news that a beggar was slowly coming down the street. Did they not think he was perhaps one of the robbers in disguise? Betty, quieting the child, crossed to the small shuttered window and gazed into the street. Her eyes widened in surprise.

Tottering toward her was the same beggar

who had accosted her and Ali Baba in the Market Place.

Eagerly she watched the man approach. She saw him pass two robed men who were gazing intently at each doorway as they strode along.

"A bite to eat," murmured the beggar, coming nearer. "Only a bite, and the blessing of Allah will descend upon you."

As the fakir halted opposite their house Betty threw back the door and motioned the man within. Slowly the beggar complied.

"Would you earn a coin?" she asked.

The beggar nodded.

"Then take a message to the palace of the Caliph. Ask for the Captain of the Guard and tell him that the Forty Thieves are patroling this street."

The beggar's eyes flashed. "This very street? Truly I thought these men were not good subjects of the Caliph." He turned to the window and glanced out. "Help is near at hand," he announced. "Even now the guards of the Caliph are stationed at each end of the street. These thieves have walked into a trap. Did they think that the Caliph would tolerate them even within the city of Bagdad!"

Ali Baba and his wife smiled faintly, disbelief in their eyes. The beggar came over to Betty.

He took from beneath his robe a long curved horn. "Go to the roof, little gypsy, and blow upon this horn. It is the signal for the capture of the robbers."

Without a word Betty took the horn and hurried up the winding stairs to the roof. Lifting the horn to her lips, she blew with all her might; then she turned to the parapet and gazed down into the street. Between the mud-walled houses a battle was in progress. She saw the robbers fleeing like pariah dogs from the soldiers of the Caliph. They had realized too late that they were bottled within the street, and now, outnumbered ten to one, they were fighting with their backs to the wall.

*The Caliph threw back his head and laughed. "For his
bravery I give him a reward."*

Betty ran down the stairs to the little group within the room. The beggar stood in the open doorway; he lifted his voice, rallying the guards in their capture of the thieves.

"Bind them securely," he called. "Take them to the dungeons!"

Betty gazed at him in amazement. He was no longer the stooping beggar; he had thrown off his tattered garments and now stood straight and tall, a handsome Arab in costly robes.

"Who—who are you?" breathed Betty.

The man's dark eyes flashed. "I am Haroun al Rashid, Caliph of Bagdad." He smiled. "I took to the streets and highways to find this robber band. Yes, I am the camel driver that Stanko found on the Great Highway yesterday. . . . With your help, little gypsy, I at last have the thieves securely bound."

Betty gasped. "You are the Caliph?"

"Yes; the gypsies are encamped within the courtyard of the palace. Come, you must join us there in a ten days' celebration of the capture of the Forty Thieves."

Betty looked round at Ali Baba and his family who had dropped to their knees in reverence and awe. "And Ali Baba?" she questioned.

The Caliph threw back his head and laughed. "For his bravery I give him a reward of twenty thousand mejidiehs. Will that do, O Driver of Donkeys?"

Ali Baba bowed again to the floor. "A thousand blessings, O Illustrious One. With the money I shall buy camels and donkeys and barter in the Market Place."

"Away with the prisoners!" commanded the Caliph to his guards. "Come, little gypsy, we go now to join the merrymakers in the palace."

SIXTH
MILE

*In Which We Journey
to Roncesvalles with
Roland and Oliver*

"*Said Olivier then, 'Our Franks are few,
And in mighty strength are the heathen crew;
Roland, Roland, yet wind one blast!
Karl will hear ere the gorge be passed.'
'I will not sound on mine ivory horn,'
Said Roland to Olivier in scorn. . . .*"

SONG OF ROLAND

I

Witches' Wood

OUTSIDE the walls of Saragossa lies a black belt of forest called Witches' Wood. The peasants shun the place by day and cross themselves with a murmured prayer when they mention it by night. Yet after a journey across the burning Spanish plain it offered to the gypsies a welcome retreat in the cool of the evening.

After supper Stanko explained its legends to Betty and Joe who sat cross-legged before the camp fire. "This is a lonely spot," he told them; "but that is why the Romanys camp here."

Joe gazed thoughtfully into the darkening forest. When presently he set out to gather firewood he made it a point to keep within earshot of the camp. The undergrowth was thick, the night dark; even the starlight was screened by the foliage above him. He had decided to go back to the van with his armload of wood, but as he turned he suddenly stopped short in alarmed surprise.

In the remote depths of the forest a light was moving.

He stared in wonderment. Who could be seeking the inmost places of Witches' Wood at that hour of night? Stanko had said that all the peasants avoided it, yet here was a torch moving far ahead. His first thought was to return at once to camp; his second, to see who traveled this silent wilderness at night. He dropped the firewood and started toward the distant light.

As he went, he saw that the light was moving also, moving ever toward the center of Witches' Wood. A profound darkness brooded over the sleeping forest. Breathless, mysterious, the heavy night air repelled yet urged him onward. He went faster, plunging by dense thickets that reached out like grasping arms to hold him, jumping over fallen tree trunks that blocked his path. Once he paused to glance back. With a start of dismay he realized that no longer could he glimpse the gypsy camp fires.

The torchlight ahead was now much nearer.

He moved forward with caution. The ground sloped here; to keep his footing, more care was needed. The air became cooler as if a mist were hovering over the damp earth; the trees, rising like gigantic shadows in black immensity, grew thicker about him. To his right some night-prowling beast lumbered noisily through the underbrush. Joe stood silent, waiting, while the blood pounded against his temples. His eyes were fixed upon the spot whence came the sound. Gradually it grew more distant, and he moved on again.

The swaying torch ahead abruptly vanished. Joe stopped. The black night seemed to press down upon him. Oh, to get back to Stanko's camp fire! But how? He had followed the torch deep into the wood; only vaguely could he remember how he had come. No—he must go on. Furtively he stumbled forward through the blackness. A dimly reflected glow on the drooping foliage told him the light was burning in some hidden nook.

The trees thinned; stars shone overhead. He saw that he had reached a hollow clearing where a fire blazed. To his left a great rock jutted out into the hollow. He crept noiselessly toward it through the slippery grass and brambles, and dropped flat on the stone. Slowly, cautiously, he wriggled forward to the edge of the bowlder. With widening eyes he gazed into the clearing.

It was a wild sight which met his gaze. The ravine lay in the remote depths of the wood, a place of gnarled trees and sinuous creeping vines. A stream, black and sluggish, threw off a mist that rose like pale wraiths to entwine the overhanging branches. But it was two figures standing impassively by the fire which caught his attention.

They were men such as he had never seen before. One was a huge, half-naked African whose ebony body glistened dully in the light. He fingered a long-handled knife stuck in his girdle. The other man was undoubtedly his master: a tall, bronzed Moor of kingly bearing, clothed in gem-studded robes of Oriental design.

Joe peered from his height, his own fears forgotten in the strangeness of these two men. He remembered what Stanko had told him of the North African Arabs, of their crossing the Strait of Gibraltar to Spain. They had conquered the languid Southern people, then had settled down to a life of ease in this land of vineyards and orange groves. More conquests had lured them, however; they had even attempted to pass through the Gates of Spain to ravage the fair land of France. But the mighty Charlemagne and his twelve noble peers had driven them back. This man, of course, was one of these Saracen conquerors, and the Negro his slave.

They were staring down the length of the ravine. Following their gaze, Joe saw that two other men were approaching. They came swiftly, their Frankish mantles flying. At the edge of the firelight they stopped.

"We have come, O Chief of the Moors," said a Frankish voice.

Joe looked closely. Where had he seen that face before? Then he remembered. It belonged to one of Charlemagne's warriors, one of his trusted captains. Why, he asked himself, had the man come to this secret meeting?

The Frank moved forward; his squire trailed behind.

"We are away from prying eyes," said the Moor with an ugly smile upon his cruel hawklike face.

The Frank nodded. "I wish to talk to you alone." He swept the forest with his glance. "Here are we safe. No one dares come to Witches' Wood. No ears will hear."

Joe's eyes grew wide; his heart throbbed in terror. He dug his toes deep into the moss and, listening quietly, drank in their plotting words.

II

The Traitor

YOU may tell Charlemagne that King Marsile will fight to the end. Never will he consent to Charlemagne's terms! Take that word to the Frankish armies, Count Ganelon, and forget it not." The Moorish Chief turned haughtily away.

The Frank strode forward with supplicating hands. "It is for that very reason that I asked for this meeting apart. Perhaps we might come to terms—you and I."

"Come to terms!" The Moor wheeled.

"Yes; what would you give me if I took back to Charlemagne words that would send him peacefully home to Aix? Would it not be worth your while?" Ganelon's crafty smile was full of hidden meaning.

The Moor threw back his head with a short, guttural laugh. "Truly, now you speak words, my Count, that are ever near to Marsile's heart. What would I give? If you carry a message, false though it be, which speeds the Frankish hosts toward the Gascony plain, then will I lay the wealth of Araby at your feet. Ten mules, all loaded with rugs and gold and amethysts, royal treasures that outshine the very jewels of Rome, shall be yours. That will I give."

"It is enough, my noble Moor. Send gifts also to the Frankish King."

"They shall go forward. But what more do you desire?" The Moor's sly smile was plainly visible to Joe.

Count Ganelon lowered his voice. "I would have you rid the army of Charlemagne's favorite —his nephew Roland, Count of the Marches of Brittany."

"The famous Roland?"

Ganelon hissed the name. "Yes, the famous Roland! For only he stands in my way to second in command. Were he killed—in sudden battle, mind you!—I, Ganelon, would be Count of the Brittany Marches."

"You hate him then?"

Count Ganelon's mouth narrowed to a thin, hard line. "I hate him!... But does that concern you, O Moor?"

Marsile laughed grimly. "How can I slay this Roland?"

"Listen: it must appear as unforeseen as a

sudden storm." Ganelon's voice sank so low that Joe had to strain his ears to catch the words. "I shall soon return and say that the Saracen chiefs will no longer invade the Frankish lands, that they will bow to the will of Charlemagne—if the armies at once leave the soil of Spain. The men are eager to return home; they will depart at once. Charles will head the main army. Roland will command a small rear guard."

"A rear guard! Ah! I begin to understand."

"I shall see that Charlemagne leads his forces through the Gates of Spain at Roncesvalles Pass—with Roland and the rear guard twenty leagues behind!"

The Moor drew closer. "And then?"

"And then, when the invaders have left the land of Spain, the Saracen warriors will flock like birds to the heights of Roncesvalles Pass. When the rear guard enters that wild gorge the Saracens will drop upon them from the crags and slay without mercy."

The Moor clenched his small hands. "I understand. Roland must never leave Spain alive."

"He must never leave Spain," Ganelon hissed agreement. "No one will suspect me. It will appear merely a sudden attack of the peasant folk."

Joe, his gaze until now intently fixed on the

two schemers, instantly noted a stir to one side of the clearing. Count Ganelon's squire rose from his seat near the huge Black and at his captain's words shrank back in horror.

"Treason!" he shrilled. "It is treason, my lord!"

The man whirled and ran toward the undergrowth.

"After him!" cried the Moor. "Get him, Mohammed!"

As the fugitive reached the edge of the clearing Joe saw the big Black leisurely draw his long, curved knife from his belt. For a second it flashed in the firelight.

Joe shuddered. A shrill cry of terror like that of a wounded animal pierced the stillness. Count Ganelon's squire fell with a crash of tearing brush. Then silence enveloped the forest.

"He will trouble us no more," laughed the Moor.

Joe buried his face in his arms to shut out sight and sound. His breath came in short, quick gasps. He dared not stir yet; he must wait—wait till these vultures had departed into the gloom whence they had come. Only then would he dare to leave his hiding place and make his way back to camp.

Camp! . . . How safe and quiet it was there

with the drowsy hum of gypsy talk amid the glow of friendly fires.

The men below him went on with their plans, but Joe did not hear. He thought only of escape. He knew what discovery meant: the flash of the Negro's long, curved knife. The minutes dragged unmercifully. Up to him still floated those traitorous hissing whispers.

Presently he realized that the men had departed. He heard the Moor and his Negro picking their way through the tangled underbrush of the forest. Ganelon had gone down the dark ravine. The fire burned low in the clearing; stars shone overhead; the brooding silence was undisturbed. He rose, tired in soul and body, and without a backward glance plunged into the forest. Not for naught had he lived with the gypsies; now the gypsy instinct guided him.

When he glimpsed far ahead through the trees the gleam of camp fires he regained his courage. His thoughts were with Charlemagne, the friend of the Romanys. The armies of France were in danger, and Roland, the hero of a nation, was blindly stepping into a trap. He had now but one desire: to get word to Roland before the traitor Ganelon returned to Roncesvalles.

III

The Rear Guard

THE green van raced over the hills toward the Spanish border. Stanko drove the sweating ponies while Betty and Joe sat on each side of him, anxiously watching the road far ahead.

"Do you think we'll overtake Ganelon?" Betty murmured.

Stanko grimly shook his head. With a rolling movement the van swung on two wheels round a curve.

Joe delightedly clutched the seat. "If only the harness doesn't break again!" he commented.

Stanko's tired face was drawn with worry. "It is an unequal race, little ones, yet must we save our friends from this hidden trap. That traitor probably rides night and day, changing horses at wayside inns. Poor Mimo and Zulieka have given their last bit of strength. I fear we have already driven them too far."

On swung the van through the noon hour,

when all Spain lies asleep. At the rise of a hill the gypsy drew the ponies to a walk.

"We should see the great high road from this hilltop," he explained. "It winds through Roncesvalles Pass. Woe to Roland and our Frankish friends if we are too late!"

The sun was still high overhead when they reached the top where Stanko halted the ponies. Eagerly the three surveyed the scene flung out like a map before them.

Directly beneath their gaze the hill fell away to a broad glen that lay somberly asleep amid surrounding mountains. Joe had expected to see the flutter of Frankish banners, the flash of armor in the sun, the dust of ten thousand marching feet; but here instead was a tranquil valley serenely resting in the shadow of the snow-capped Pyrenees. Opposite them great crags rose gaunt and stately against a turquoise sky.

"That is the road, and there is Roncesvalles Pass," said Stanko as he pointed to a thin line that pierced the mountains to the east. "The road winds through a gorge to the plains of Gascony."

"But where are Charlemagne's armies?" Joe broke in.

Stanko thoughtfully surveyed the valley. "I fear we are too late. The place seems deserted."

"Too late!" cried Betty in dismay.

"Yes; see the haze hovering above the gorge? An army has passed through there this very day."

Joe gazed through a blue mist to the left. "Stanko, can't you see a camp on the hillside?"

"A mere cluster of tents!" cried Stanko. "Surely only a few hundred men. Can that be Roland's rear guard?" His voice lowered to a mournful note.

"We must tell him, Stanko," Joe entreated. "We must warn him that the Moors will attack when he enters the Pass."

The gypsy jumped to the ground and patted the tired ponies. "Mimo and Zulieka can go no farther. Yet I cannot leave Betty here alone. Could you go, little master?"

"Yes, let me go! It won't take long. Where will you wait?"

"Here. We shall make camp on this hillside. Take the news to Roland and tell him to speed after the armies. He may yet make Roncesvalles before the Saracens approach."

Joe set off toward the distant camp. He had little difficulty in keeping the line of tents in view, for only rocks and bowlders studded the hillside. It was late in the afternoon before he was halted by two sentries of Roland's outpost.

He explained his errand and was immediately ordered to proceed under guard. As the soldier led the way through the Frankish camp Joe looked with interest at the brown tents with banners flying, at Charlemagne's mail-clad warriors seated on the ground at their evening meal.

A group of soldiers looked up as Joe passed. "Ho! Who goes there?" shouted one, setting down his goblet of wine.

"A gypsy lad," answered the guard. "He desires to see our lord, Roland."

"Bring the lad here, guardsman! Let us question him first. Perhaps he's merely some lying impostor."

The sentinel waved the men aside. "We go to Count Roland's tent. Away, varlets, lest the captain hear you!"

A half-drunken soldier swayed to his feet. "Bring him here. 'Tis long since any merriment entered the camp. A ducking in the pond would bring forth the truth."

He lunged toward Joe.

"What means this?"

Like the quick snap of a whip the question brought the group to attention. Joe turned and beheld a youthful warrior regarding them sternly.

"A messenger, my lord, whom I was bringing to Count Roland's tent."

"And these drunken louts interfered?" The man's wrath was plainly evident. "Is this the way Frankish soldiers carouse when they act as rear guard to Charlemagne's armies? Do they not know that we remain in enemy land?" His voice swelled in anger. "Chain these men to the baggage wagons where they belong!"

As a half-dozen soldiers sprang forward at his bidding, he turned to Joe and his glance softened. "Have you news, my lad? Come to Count Roland's tent."

Without another word he led the way. Joe gratefully followed.

"It is Count Roland's friend, Oliver," whispered the guardsman.

At the large-domed tent he stopped and held aside the flap. In the pallid light of the interior Joe discerned a mail-clad figure seated at a table. The man looked up at his entrance.

"What is it, Oliver?"

"The men tire of Spain, my friend. They would make merry at a messenger's expense; this gypsy lad brings news."

Count Roland rose. "My men interfere with a messenger? I hope you punished them. Severely?"

"Justly, I think."

Roland's kindly eyes took in the young messenger before him. "What tidings, my lad? Speak."

Joe stood first on one foot, then on the other. This man who faced him was Roland, hero of the Franks, a fighter of renown, and the subject of innumerable minstrels' lays. And now a plot had been skillfully laid to entrap him. The thought of the man's danger spurred Joe to speech; his words tumbled forth.

Roland and Oliver quietly listened. As Joe continued with his story of the meeting in Witches' Wood, of the Saracen Chief and the coming of Ganelon, of their treachery and the squire's death, the two men's brows grew black.

"Treason!" Oliver breathed.

Count Roland strode across the floor. "This means death to traitorous Ganelon!"

"We must not be caught in Roncesvalles Pass," broke in Oliver. "Give the order to march. We must go this very night."

"Shall we flee like so many mice?"

"Not flight, my lord, but our men's lives must not be thrown away."

"It is true, my Oliver. Give the order to make ready."

Joe heard the order passed down the line of tents: "Make ready! We march to-night!"

Roland paced the floor till his friend returned.

"A brave lad to bring us this information," Oliver pronounced. "Your warning has saved our lives, for now we shall be ready." He crossed to Roland. "It is not too late to ask aid of Charlemagne. Blow your horn, Roland! The Franks will hear through Roncesvalles Pass and return to our support."

Roland wheeled in scorn. "We shall be ready for the heathen. There is no need to ask help of Charles."

Oliver put his hand on the other's shoulder. "Always are you headstrong, my friend; sometimes I think you have more pride than caution. Think, Roland! The Saracens may outnumber us ten to one. Would you risk that? Wind your horn, Roland! Charles will hear."

"Never!" Roland smote the table with an angry fist. "I shall not ask aid of Charles! And perhaps, Oliver, we shall meet no Saracens."

Joe saw Oliver's face grow tense. It was not from fear, he reflected, but rather from the thought of their few hundred men so near to home and yet so far; for now, like an approaching thunderclap, this new danger threatened. Oliver was more wary, more thoughtful, the boy perceived, than the veteran fighter, Roland.

"Yes," continued the latter, "perhaps we shall not see a single Moor. Would you have me laughed at by the peers of Charlemagne?"

Even as Roland said the words, he abruptly stopped. He flung back his head, listening. Joe saw his hand clutch the table, saw his mouth grow grim. For, rising tremulously on the evening air, there came the distant sound of beating drums.

"The Saracens approach!" cried Oliver. "Wind your horn, Roland! Charles will hear."

Roland's fist again smote the table. "Never! First shall we fight!"

With pounding pulses Joe listened. The tent, still as a yawning grave, seemed to tremble from that distant soft vibration. Steadily advancing from east and west, from north and south, there came the throbbing note of drums—the pagan drums of war.

IV

Roncesvalles

AS UNEXPECTEDLY as it had begun, the rhythmic beat of heathen drums melted away beyond the hills, leaving the stillness of the evening air even more alarming than the sound itself. The troops of the rear guard made ready for their march through Roncesvalles. Tents were loaded upon the unwieldy wooden carts, soldiers mounted their pawing steeds, orders flew down the line from company commanders.

Joe, watching the busy scene, wondered how he was to return to the green van on the distant hill without meeting Saracen detachments. Yet the enemy's advance guard had not yet made an appearance. Scouts had returned with the word that the enemy was still several leagues away.

Oliver touched Joe's shoulder. "Wait, lad," he said, "I may have further need of you."

Joe saw him cross to Roland, who was conversing with his officers. A moment later the two leaders came his way, talking together in low tones.

"Be not so foolish," Oliver implored. "Have you no desire to see gentle France again? Wind your horn! Take it from your shoulder and make it ring through Roncesvalles Pass. Charlemagne——"

"Stop!" Indignation flamed in Roland's eyes. "Do not presume too much upon our friendship. I will not call for help! Say no more."

"As you will."

Oliver turned on his heel and motioned to Joe. Near the line of baggage wagons he paused. "I must beg your help," he whispered.

"Yes?" murmured Joe.

"I cannot move him," Oliver sighed; "yet do I feel that he is headstrong—as ever. Many times has Charles warned him that his valor would get the better of his caution. Many times, too, have I besought him and won him over to more prudent ways. But to-day he is immovable. He endangers his brave men's lives."

Oliver's gaze swept the line of troops. "Neither will he allow me to send ahead a messenger. You, lad, may leave the camp, and he will think nothing amiss."

"You want me——"

"Yes, you! I will give you my own swift

mount. Ride to Charles with word of our danger. Tell him of Ganelon's treachery. I beg of you—do not refuse! Will you go?"

"But how, Oliver? How?"

"Ride straight down the road through Roncesvalles. The Saracens have not yet come. Charlemagne will send help to meet us within the gorge."

Joe nodded assent. His eyes searched the hills that bordered the valley; he half expected to see the enemy appear from behind the rocks and shower Saracen spears upon him. Oliver led forward a small riding horse. Joe took in his perfect lines with delight. He jumped into the saddle and patted his mount. What fun to ride such a horse! And yet—suppose a Moorish knife came whirring through the air! He shuddered.

"Ride swiftly," implored Oliver. "Ride like the wind! Charles must know of our danger."

Joe guided his horse through the littered camp. At the edge he glanced back to see if Roland were visible, but he could not make him out. Then putting spurs to his mount, he rode in a swift, smooth gallop along the road toward the mountains.

The way was deserted; the cool evening air was caressingly fresh on his brow. Ahead, the Pyrenees loomed mistily through the haze.

"Faster—faster!" he urged his steed.

The horse responded with the easy swing of a thoroughbred. Wild straggling bushes fell away behind him. The mountains loomed closer; the purple of their crags deepened.

Dusk approached. As the highroad entered the dark defile of Roncesvalles he heard the hoof beats of the lone horse echoing from cliff to cliff as if a hundred Saracens were swiftly following in the remote folds of the mountains. Then he realized that above the steady beat of his horse's hoofs another sound was audible. The distant throb of Saracen drums rose and fell within the narrow gorge.

He turned in his saddle and glanced back. Far down the valley the rear guard marched toward him, but between them, lining the hills, the mountains, the crags, flashed a multitude of spears.

The pass swarmed with Moors.

Joe looked up. Far above, dark forms flitted like shadows from rock to rock. Spurring his horse, he leaned close to the flying mane and rode for his very life.

A spear hummed overhead. Another followed. The deep shadows of the rocks seemed to peer at him as he galloped past. He gazed ahead, wondering if he had escaped all the advance guard of the Saracen host. The wind whistled down the pass with a low, mournful wail. A drop of rain fell. He pulled his coat close about him.

It was now so dark that he could not even glimpse the road. Loosing his hold on the bridle rein, he dug his heels into his horse's flanks—he would trust his mount to keep to the road. With the hum of a rising wind in his ears, he plunged on through the velvet darkness.

V

The Horn

DAWN raced to meet him at the narrow Gate of Spain.

He pulled up his horse and gazed through the early mist. A bank of cloud still hovered over the Pyrenees, but the Gascony plain lay soft and green in the mellow light. Strewn on the open country like the pattern of an Eastern rug were the tents of Charlemagne's army.

He pushed on with renewed eagerness and, when a sentry halted him, almost fell from his mount from sheer exhaustion. He observed that fires were kindled about the tents, that preparations were under way for the day's march northward. So eager was he to divulge his information that he hardly noticed the curious eyes leveled his way as he was led to the royal tent. There near the camp fire, surrounded by his captains, stood Charlemagne.

"Roland needs help!"

Joe thought he was shouting, but the words barely escaped his lips.

Charlemagne motioned him closer. "A message from Roland?"

A murmur of dismay went round the group of warriors. Joe noted Charlemagne's face blanch above his beard, saw the sudden light of apprehension glow in his eyes. Did Charlemagne remember St. Remy?

Joe swayed slightly as he stood there before the group. "Roland is surrounded. He refused to send for help, but Oliver bade me ride with the news."

"Surrounded!" Charlemagne's deep voice thundered across the circle. "Surrounded? By whom?"

"By the Saracens."

"The Saracens!" He paused in amazed disbelief. "But that is impossible. We made a truce. Roland was to follow twenty leagues behind. Would the Saracens dare attempt treachery?"

A tall, thin captain stepped forward. Joe almost cried aloud in sudden anger. The man was Ganelon. In vivid detail he recalled the scene in Witches' Wood.

"Do not believe him, sire," Ganelon's suave voice murmured. "Who is this upstart, anyway? Who is he to bring word from Count Roland of

Brittany! Why was not a Frankish messenger sent?"

"It is strange——"

"It is doubly strange, sire," Ganelon went on; "for had Roland needed help he would have blown his horn, and our outposts would have heard."

Joe perceived a smile upon the man's lips. It stung him to action.

"It is true!" he cried. "Look—Oliver gave me his very own horse to ride. Even as I came through the pass, I saw the enemy making ready to attack."

"Sire, do not believe it. This braggart is a stranger."

"It is true," again affirmed Joe. "It is treachery too—treachery within your ranks."

"Treason within my ranks? I cannot believe it."

"Yet it is the truth! Five nights ago in a wood near Saragossa I saw——"

Ganelon strode forward and motioned to a sentinel. Hands gripped Joe from behind.

"Away with him," ordered Ganelon. "Should the peers of France listen to the lying words of a gypsy braggart?"

Joe's aching body trembled with rage. To have ridden all night through Roncesvalles' dark defile for help, and then to be distrusted. It was incredible. Tears moistened his lashes. He looked round the little circle. The faces of the warriors were sternly skeptical. Only Charlemagne's eyes were kind.

"I cannot believe that my emissary to King Marsile would be guilty of treason," said Charlemagne.

With despair Joe perceived that no one believed him. The sentinel was already leading him away.

"Send the urchin to the chief of the kitchen train," called Ganelon.

Joe hardly noted the words. He was thinking of Roland facing the enemy in the dawn, surrounded, outnumbered ten to one; and he was now unable to bring assistance. Like an eel he slipped from his captor's grasp. Swinging about, he ran to Charlemagne.

"You must believe me," he gasped. "It is true —every word! Don't you remember St. Remy— you believed me then!"

Charlemagne regarded him long and steadily. Joe, unflinchingly returning the gaze, saw the man's face change. A kindly expression spread over the stern countenance of the warrior; recognition flashed in his eyes. A faint flicker of a smile showed that he remembered how splendidly they had outwitted the barbarian at St. Remy.

Nervously Ganelon laughed. "Is it my word against a gypsy's?" he snarled. "Would you believe him first?"

"Not a gypsy's word, my Ganelon, but the word of Sir Joseph, who was knighted by my hand at St. Remy as a token of our gratitude for saving the Castle."

Charlemagne's eyes narrowed to mere slits. His voice was harsh. "I never yet have had cause to believe treachery of a Frankish baron, yet I feel that Sir Joseph speaks the truth. Tell me, Ganelon, whence came those mules laden with silver and rugs which you brought back with you?"

"Gifts, sire. Half for you and half for me as your messenger."

"For you, Count Ganelon, a lordly gift!"

"He speaks falsely," Joe broke in. "The gypsy camp was on the edge of Witches' Wood. I saw Ganelon meet Marsile, the Saracen Chief, and plot to surround the rear guard—to kill Roland."

"To kill Roland!" Charlemagne's voice rose. "To kill my favorite nephew? If this be true, my captain, horses shall drag you through the camp till you die."

Joe perceived that the traitor's face went suddenly white. A flood of words broke from the boy's lips. "I saw his squire struck down by Marsile's Negro, because the man cried out at the treachery of the plot."

"Send the urchin away," snarled Ganelon. "Did I not tell you that the man fell from his horse and was killed!"

Charlemagne nodded. "It sounds so very simple, Ganelon of Bordeaux—so very plausible."

Abruptly Joe became aware that the little group was listening. Their eyes were raised toward the mountain pass; they seemed to be hearing some distant sound. His heart almost stopped beating.

"Roland's horn!" Charlemagne gasped the words.

Joe heard it then, the merest echo of a blast like a long-drawn cry piercing the stillness of the pass of Roncesvalles. His glance came back to Ganelon. The man was quivering with fright; he slunk away like an outcast, his clawlike hands extended.

"Traitor!" shouted Charlemagne. "Roland would never blow his horn unless he were in direst need. Seize him, my men! Chain him!"

Quick orders went down the line. "Mount—mount! Ride for Roncesvalles!"

With trembling hands Charlemagne drew on his helmet.

"Woe to me! Why did I not recognize you at once! Hurry—hurry! Come, my lad. You must tell me all while we ride to Roland's aid."

VI

The Battle

HALFWAY through Roncesvalles Pass
they heard again the sound of Roland's
horn.

"A second time? He weakens!" muttered the
soldiers as they spurred their mounts. "Surely
the rear guard is in dire straits."

Joe pulled his horse to the roadside and dismounted. The last few riders of the Frankish host
galloped past. He watched them out of sight;
then, unbridling his mount, he let him graze at
will. It was damp and cool within the gorge;
he made a camp fire and, exhausted, lay down
near it. Here he would wait till the army returned.

All through the day he slept fitfully. In his
ears was the distant hum of the raging battle.

He wondered if Charlemagne had arrived in
time. With throbbing heart he recalled the sound
of that last weak blast, so weak that he could
almost see the tired Roland winding his horn.

He pictured the battle in the Pass: the few hundred Franks of the rear guard, outnumbered ten to one, still bravely facing their foe; the steady beating down of their resistance by the Saracen hordes; Oliver, perhaps weak from loss of blood, imploring Roland to sound one blast; Roland finally yielding—finally lifting the horn to his lips to send the echoes ringing through the gorge; then the steady flash of spears, and another weak, gurgling blast.

From time to time Joe rose and nervously glanced down the road. No approaching horseman cheered him, however. He paced wearily back and forth. The leaden day dragged slowly to its end.

An unexpected noise roused him. He must have been asleep. Raising himself on his elbow, he listened.

The unmistakable patter of horses' hoofs floated down the Pass. Trembling, he rose, crossed to the middle of the road, and waited.

Mimo and Zulieka brought the green van swinging round a curve. His surprise gave way to joy; breathless, he ran to meet them. He dimly saw Betty and Stanko on the seat.

Something in the set faces of the two, as they approached, struck him into silence. Abruptly he stopped and waited by the roadside. An iron weight seemed to pull at his heart.

"What—what happened?" he stammered in anguish. "Didn't Charlemagne get there in time?"

As he looked at Betty he saw that her face was wet with tears.

"Well? . . ."

Stanko dropped the reins. "Charlemagne's armies are pursuing the Saracens toward Saragossa. But he arrived too late. The rear guard made a brave fight against overwhelming odds."

For the length of a dozen heartbeats Joe stared at him; then his glance wavered and traveled up the silent Pass of Roncesvalles. "Roland—and Oliver? . . . I didn't get through the pass in time?"

"You did nobly, little master," broke in Stanko. "'Twas no fault of yours, for you did your very best. If all our efforts were to end in victory we should never know the joy of achievement."

Stanko eyed the reins grimly. In a firmer voice he went on: "Charlemagne found the heathen fled. Oliver was stretched on the hillside, and near him with his face toward Spain lay Roland.

"Charles is weeping in despair. He is an old man now, and peace should be his due, yet it is ever fight—fight! He knows not how he will tell Aude the Fair when he returns to Aix. When she asks, 'Where is Roland?' how can he say, 'He sleeps in Spanish soil'? . . ."

Speechless, Joe clambered to his seat.

Stanko flicked the reins. "On, Mimo! On, Zulieka! This dank air makes me shiver."

Betty dashed the tears from her eyes. "Where do we go now, Stanko?"

"We go south. Do you not see how approaching winter has chilled our hearts? Yes, we go south to seek warmer climes."

"*Within the garden of Beaucaire*
He met her by a secret stair.
The night was centuries ago . . .
'Come with me now, my love, my pet,'
Said Aucassin to Nicolette."

STEDMAN

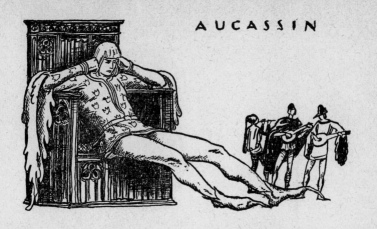

I

Maytime in Provence

THE caravan leisurely swung through
France to lands of summer by the sea.
One spring morning found the gypsies
encamped on a poppy-covered hill below a grove
of poplars. Across a broad vineyard rose the
town and castle of Beaucaire.

"It is a kindly land, this land of the South,"
remarked Stanko.

"Yes, the vines are already full of grapes,"
commented Betty, who was seated on the grass
beside Toto the Bear. "The peasants told me
the Tokays would soon be red as rubies. Toto
didn't want to wait; he ate some green ones, and
now he won't move."

CASTLE OF BEAUCAIRE

She stroked the bear's dark mane. Toto, however, failed to take notice; stretched in the shade
of a poplar, he lay with closed eyes.

"Bears are ever greedy, little one. By nightfall
he should be well again."

When Joe arrived with an armful of wood the

old gypsy at once built the fire. Betty busied herself with the tidying up of the van. She was interrupted at her work of sweeping the steps by the approach of a tall man garbed in the purple and green livery of the Castle of Beaucaire.

"I come from Count Garin, O Gypsies," said the stranger. "The Count desires the presence at his Castle of the jongleurs and fortune tellers of your tribe."

Stanko nodded. "We Romanys are ever willing to entertain a lord as great as the Count of Beaucaire. When does he wish us there?"

"At once. The heir to this fief of Beaucaire, the young Aucassin, despairs as if he were one-and-eighty instead of one-and-twenty. He sits all day with somber brow; nothing pleases him. Even the troubadours and jesters of the court cannot make him smile."

Betty saw that the Count's messenger was talkative. As his eyes lighted upon Toto he paused.

"The bear perhaps has some tricks?"

"Oh, many tricks," said Betty, with pride in her voice. "He walks on his hind feet and balances a mug of wine upon his nose."

"Then truly he is the one to make my young lord Aucassin laugh. Bring him; in return he shall have a goodly supper."

"Little master," queried Stanko, "think you he will perform to-night?"

Joe rubbed Toto's nose with a poplar leaf. "Of course; he is only lazy in the warm sun. Up, Toto. Up!"

The bear yawned and rose to his ungainly height. As Joe sent him through his antics the messenger loudly applauded. "Aye, a goodly sight," he chuckled; "surely my lord Aucassin will smile at this rare creature."

"Meg the Fortune Teller shall go with us," said Stanko. "She will tell what future awaits this young lord. Make ready, little ones. We shall be guests of the Count of Beaucaire."

As Betty donned her gayest gypsy frock she reflected that if the sad young lord of the Castle could see Toto just once he would surely laugh.

When a half hour later they stood in the great tapestried hall of the Castle she was not, however, so confident. About a long table laden with roasted peacock, ginger, fruit, and spiced wine were seated the lords and ladies, all laughing merrily at the bear's antics; but one man sat apart with a scowl upon his handsome face. This was Aucassin, the only son of the aged Count of Beaucaire.

Betty thought him good to look at, but much too sad. He was as melancholy as a rainy afternoon. Quietly she drew near his seat by the great fireplace. He did not notice her, however; his blond head was bowed in his hands.

Old Count Garin, putting down his empty goblet, gazed in anger toward his son. "What!" he rasped. "Still scowling as if all the world were making war upon you?"

Aucassin lifted his head. His hands were clenched. "Is it not as if all the world were at war against me? It is five days since I have seen Nicolette."

The Count's fist banged upon the table. "What! You again dare to mention that maid, the child of a mere merchant of the town? Forget her. You must marry a maiden who is at least the daughter of a duke or a count."

Aucassin rose and faced his angry parent. "There is no place so high in all the world," he gravely said, "but that my Nicolette would grace it well. Were she Queen of France or Empress of all the East I could not love her more. She is Nicolette the Fair—and none other will I marry!"

Count Garin, blustering and fuming, pounded the table. "Never! Never shall you marry her! Let no more be said." He turned to his goblet.

Betty noted how white and strained was Aucassin's face as he dropped back to his bench.

Meg the Fortune Teller shuffled across the room toward him.

"Let me read your future, young man," chirped the old gypsy woman, her keen eyes searching Aucassin's face. "The stars tell us that mere mortals can say neither yea nor nay."

She hovered like a crow above his hand. "I see winds blowing bitter cold and the flash of a storm surrounding you."

She paused, and Aucassin's dark brow grew darker still.

"Yet the stars in their courses are ever kind to those of great faith. Behold! I see you married to a maiden of wondrous beauty."

" 'Tis Nicolette!" cried Aucassin. " 'Tis she!"

Count Garin again rose with flaming eyes. "What is this you say? Never shall my son marry a merchant's daughter! This is not true love; he only thinks it is. Away, hag, lest I set the hounds upon you!"

Meg slunk away to a corner behind the fireplace.

"My son, Aucassin," went on the Count, "before such an impossible marriage takes place I shall throw you into the dungeons and banish this maid from the land."

He dropped to his seat and wiped the moisture from his brow. The ladies whispered together.

Betty, with a fearful glance about to make sure that she was unobserved, slipped over to the unhappy Aucassin. Just one word of sympathy would she say to him.

"He is cruel," she said softly. "When to-day we passed the great house of the merchant-captain I saw at a window a beautiful maid. Our guide told us she was the fair Nicolette."

"You saw her?" Aucassin forgot his father's wrath. "Tell me how she appeared."

"She was gazing across the vineyards toward the olive groves. She did not move. I think she was listening to the convent bells."

Aucassin sat with pensive eyes. "It was she. . . . It was Nicolette!" He glanced about. The people were again occupied with their wine.

"My father no longer deserves obedience. He thinks it is not true love, but I will show him that it is! Tell me, will you carry a message to the fair Nicolette?"

"A message?" Betty paused uncertainly.

"Yes, to her. You said you pitied me. I know that you pity her, for no one could see my Nicolette and not love her. Her eyes are blue as Venetian skies, and her hair like flaming gold. Take her this message: 'Be at the garden end of the secret stair at the rise of the moon to-night!'"

Betty hesitated. Quickly she swept the hall

with her glance. She and the young lord of Beaucaire were now unnoticed by the members of the company, who were gayly tossing nimble-witted jests across the table. Would she dare to take this word to the fair Nicolette? She looked at Aucassin. His face was eager with hope. She nodded.

Aucassin touched his lips as a sign for secrecy. "I will be forever in your debt, little gypsy." No longer was his face shrouded in gloom. He smiled. "You will know the house; it is the great dwelling of the merchant-captain. You have the message?"

Betty repeated it. "Aucassin sends this word: 'Be at the garden end of the secret stair at moonrise to-night.' Now I must go."

She slipped quietly over to Stanko. Aucassin's glance followed her as if he suddenly saw far ahead in the darkness a faintly dawning star.

II

The Secret Stair

AT THE far end of the Street of the Gardens lay the great house of the merchant-captain. Betty lifted the knocker, and a dull thud echoed on the quiet evening air. The door slowly opened, disclosing a black-eyed maid.

"What is it you desire?" she questioned.

"I should like to see Nicolette."

"Mademoiselle Nicolette is not at home to visitors." The girl, bobbing a curtsey, made as if to close the door.

"Oh, don't," Betty begged. "I must see Mademoiselle. I have a message from a dear friend."

"Why did you not say so in the first place? That is different. Come in."

Betty followed her into a long, dark hallway where the maid motioned her to wait. She reappeared a few minutes later and said: "Mademoiselle awaits you upstairs."

In the upper passage she knocked upon a door. Betty heard a soft voice answer, and the wench swung open the door.

As Betty entered the room her first impression was one of luxurious splendor and charm. Tapestries adorned the walls; heavy curtains swayed before the windows open to the twilight. Through the casement came the fragrant odors of the garden: rose and lilac, heliotrope and jasmine.

From the window seat a slender girl rose; her fragile beauty was silhouetted against the evening sky. Betty gazed in admiration. Aucassin had said that Nicolette's eyes were blue as the sky reflected in the calm waters of the Adriatic and her hair the color of gold. She was even more lovely than this.

"That will do, Francine." The latter went out with a little slam of the door.

"What is it?" Nicolette eagerly queried. "You say you come from a friend?"

Betty smiled; here she felt herself upon enchanted ground. "To-day I was in the Castle of the Count of Beaucaire. Aucassin gave me a message for you."

"Aucassin!" There was rapture in her voice. "How looked he? What did he say? Is he coming to see me?"

"He gave me this message: 'Tell the fair Nicolette to meet me at the garden end of the secret stair at moonrise to-night.'"

"In the garden at rise of moon," Nicolette

dwelt lovingly upon the words. "Tell me more! How looked he? Is he well? Does his father relent?"

She drew Betty to the seat by the open window where she plied her with questions. There they sat and talked, while the garden scents, blown on the breeze, were wafted up to them.

"You shall stay for supper," said Nicolette at last. "I must eat in my room now by order of my father. He is fond of Aucassin, but he must obey the Count of Beaucaire in this. So he has instructed that wench, Francine, to watch me like a hawk. I cannot gaze from the window that she is not here at my elbow. Oh, it is intolerable! But we shall see Aucassin to-night. You must watch the house for us."

After supper Nicolette and Betty impatiently waited for the moon to rise. They stood at the open casement, talking in low tones, and watched the night breeze playing among the roses in the garden. At the first glimpse of the moon's rim above the garden wall Nicolette took Betty's hand and led her down the corridor to a low window which opened upon a small stairway.

As Betty followed down the steps she heard the voices of servants gossiping in the scullery. Nicolette's hand tightened upon hers. Across the green turf, bordered by beds of pansies, they went till an ivy-covered wall blocked their path. Here the evening primroses made a blot of vivid yellow against the green.

"Keep watch here," whispered Nicolette. "I go to the corner. There lies a secret stair now unused. It connects with a lane that leads to the Market Place."

She passed swiftly along the wall, skirted a bed of crocuses, and paused in the deep shadow of the corner. Betty saw her pull aside a clump of ivy and swing back a wooden door. The stairs were evidently deserted, for she crossed to a small bench beside the shrubbery and sat down to wait.

In silence Betty watched. A cricket chirruped from the path; fireflies flitted amid the shrubs; a lilac tree enveloped her in its fragrant perfume. Slowly the moon stole over the wall; its radiant sheen drenched the garden with a silver mist. Objects stood out clearly now. A woman came from the kitchen door and stood gazing over the garden toward the wall.

Betty shrank back into the shadows. Her pulses pounded in her ears. Did the servant see her? Evidently not, for she soon turned and re-entered the lighted doorway.

A dark shadow flitted across the turf. Betty almost cried aloud in fright. Then she saw that

"Keep watch here," whispered Nicolette

it was Aucassin. He had entered the garden by the secret stair. Nicolette rose and advanced to meet him.

A nightingale began his low song from a hedge so close that Betty thought were she to put forth her hand she might touch it. The velvet notes merged into the faint night echoes of the moonlit garden. She stood entranced before its haunting beauty, oblivious of all else. She had utterly forgotten her post as guard for Aucassin and Nicolette.

Somewhere behind her an owl hooted. Another took up its weird, strange cry from the street. The song of the nightingale was instantly stilled. Startled, Betty waited uncertainly. A third cry of an owl sounded from the servants' entrance.

Behind Betty footsteps grated upon the gravel. She whirled in sudden terror.

Too late she realized her plight. Before she could cry out a word of warning, before she could make an effort toward flight, arms seized her. A hand was swiftly drawn across her mouth. She struggled madly. She tore and scratched at her captors. A low chuckle was the only answer. Disheartened, she lay limp with her eyes fixed upon the scene before her.

"Seize them!" a man's hoarse voice shouted.

In a flash the garden was alive with men.

Betty saw Aucassin and Nicolette start for the stairs. Dark forms blocked their way. Like swooping hawks the men were upon them. Nicolette's hands were fastened behind her, but she defiantly faced her captors with her breast heaving and her eyes flashing scorn. Aucassin's labored efforts to wrench himself free proved futile. Four guardsmen imprisoned him in their brutal grasp. With arms pinioned to his sides, he gazed across the moonlit space at his Nicolette.

"We have him, my lord!"

"Hold him well." The tall form of Count Garin strode past Betty. "For this, my disobedient son, you shall lie in the dungeons till you repent."

"Sir," said Aucassin, his repressed rage struggling with calm, "I would tell you again: I intend to marry my Nicolette!" His glance crossed to Nicolette. He drew a long breath and smiled encouragingly. "We should have fled this very night!" he cried. "Yes, this very night."

"Never shall you see each other again!" rasped the Count. "My Captain, let your daughter be seen no more in Beaucaire."

The Captain bowed his head. "It will be done, my lord."

"My son shall trouble this house no longer. Take him away, varlets. To the dungeons!"

Nicolette wrenched at the hands that bound

her. Her face was white with fear. "No—no! Not there," she wailed. "My father shall send me from the land. Do not lock my Aucassin within the earth."

"Silence! I am Count of Beaucaire."

Betty's captor loosed his hold. "What shall we do with this small child?" he muttered.

"Small child!" thought Betty. "Oh, I hate you."

She ran to Nicolette and held her close as if she would protect her from these cruel guardsmen. "Forgive me," she sobbed; "I did not see them come."

Nicolette murmured words of comfort, but her eyes were dimmed with tears.

"Remember, my Nicolette," came Aucassin's voice as they led him away, "no matter where they hide you, yet will I search you out."

Betty heard the Count raging among his men. "Farewell, my Captain," he said to Nicolette's father. "My lord Aucassin goes to the dungeons. A veil at the holy convent of Roche de Frêne would hide your daughter well."

"Yes, my lord." The merchant-captain turned to his men. "Lock that child and my daughter in her room! To-morrow they shall be banished from the land. Away with them!"

III

The Escape

BETTY awoke with a start. Where was
she? This was not the friendly darkness
of the green van with its little window
open at her side. This was a room of vast obscurity.

She sat up in bed. Of course! She was in Nicolette's great four-poster and there opposite her
was the long high window with the moonlight
pouring into the room.

"Awake, little gypsy," a low voice whispered.
"Awake!"

"Nicolette, you startled me!" She grasped the
hand of the girl bending over her.

"Hush! Not so loud." Nicolette raised her
hand; her touch on Betty's lips was as soft, as
caressing as the fluttering wings of a butterfly.
"We must flee, little one. Hurry and dress."

She leaned nearer. "The door is locked from
the outside. Francine sleeps in the next room.
Caution is needed!"

"But how are we to escape, Nicolette?"

"Through the window. 'Tis the only way. Dangerous it is, yet must we try it, for I dare not wait till to-morrow. Neither do I dare leave you here to face my angry sire in the morning. I know not what he or the Count will do."

As Betty dressed, Nicolette dragged the coverlets to the window where, one by one, she knotted them together.

"What! Do we slide down those?" Betty's voice was full of concern.

Nicolette grimly nodded. "Not so loud, little one. The ground is not far below, and this makeshift rope will reach. Come!"

After tying one end of the coverlets to the pillar in the window, she dropped the long line over the casement. Then she and Betty stood silent, listening. The profound quiet of the house remained unbroken. The night was serene and clear; the moonlight lay like molten silver upon the garden. In the lilac bush below the window the wind was singing, and across the turf a nightingale warbled from the hedge.

"Francine sleeps like a Crusader upon the march," whispered Nicolette. "Who shall go first?"

"You lead. I'll follow."

Nicolette wrapped a sea-blue mantle about her and stepped to the ledge. As she firmly grasped the ropelike sheets, Betty breathlessly watched. Carefully, slowly, Nicolette let herself down the heavy cord.

Betty leaned out the window. Nicolette had reached the ground and now looked up to her and waved. What a distance it was! What if one of the coverlets came untied!

"Come!" motioned Nicolette.

With throbbing heart, Betty firmly grasped the heavy rope. It was strong. Of course it would hold. As she swung out into the void she thought for a second she was falling. Her feet touched the wall, and she gained courage. Carefully she slid downward, hand under hand, as she had seen Joe do many times. Then she had thought it such an easy thing to do; now she knew how tremendously difficult it was.

Her gypsy slippers clung to the mossy stones of the wall. Her arms grew tired and numb. How they ached! Could she hold long enough? When Nicolette's upraised hands steadied her she caught her breath in a sob of joy. But her face, turned to her companion, was strong with fortitude and achievement.

"Bravely done, little gypsy. Follow me."

On tiptoe Nicolette led the way across the turf, ever keeping in the shadow of tree or hedge. As she followed, Betty perceived that the dew lay heavy upon the grass and that the daisies glistened with a thousand points of light. At the corner of the garden Nicolette drew back the wooden door.

"The secret stair," she whispered.

A light suddenly flashed across the garden. Nicolette grasped the door for support.

"Francine—she is awake!"

A torch was blazing in Nicolette's open window. Betty glimpsed a woman's dark form leaning over the casement. Before they could move, a shrill voice pierced the stillness.

"Escape! Master! Master, they have fled!"

Nicolette deftly closed the gate behind them. "Quick! We must run for it."

Taking Betty's hand, she darted down the short flight of steps to the lane. Here on the left the houses stood hushed and clear in the mellow light, and those on the right in deepest shadow as if, like a saber, the moonlight had cleaved the street in twain.

They chose the shadowed wall and sped on slippered feet toward the Market Place. Behind them they heard the mounting hue and cry.

Betty's hand flew to her breast. A guard must have seen them take to the lane. Shouts that grew steadily nearer followed them. Nicolette glanced back; Betty heard her gasp.

The shouts increased.. Betty threw a quick glance over her shoulder. Their pursuers were rapidly gaining. Dark forms, plainly visible in the moonlight, were racing toward them.

"Make the Market Place and we're safe," Nicolette gasped.

Closer came the pursuit. Muffled footsteps speeding after them grew louder. On down the twisting lane they ran. Betty's heart was pounding like the steady beat of a war drum; Nicolette too, she saw, was frantic with fear. Why didn't they take to a side lane? They would be caught here. It was only a matter of moments now. To make the Market Place with its nooks and dark crannies and intersecting streets was clearly impossible.

"Nicolette," she called softly. "Take a side road."

On they sped. Their pursuers gained steadily. Suddenly a street opened in the shadow to the right. Into this they darted, turned again, and doubled back toward the house of the merchant-captain.

Abruptly Nicolette stopped and, trembling from head to foot, drew Betty into the darkness of a doorway. There without a word they crouched. A lone pursuer pattered down the street toward the town square. In the sanctuary of the doorway the two fugitives clung to each other while the unsuspecting guardsman, oblivious of the nearness of his quarry, ran noisily past.

They heard the distant shouts of the searchers in the Market Place. Betty peered down the street where torches cast a fitful glow over the stalls in which the peasants were wont to display their wares on market days. Apparently they had eluded their pursuers. She had regained her breath; Nicolette, too, was once more eager with hope.

"We must start again," Nicolette whispered.

"The gypsy camp is in the poplar grove on the hillside," Betty explained. "You will be safe there. How can we reach it?"

"There is a postern gate near the Castle." Nicolette paused thoughtfully. "I wish I might speak with Aucassin——"

"Speak with Aucassin! How can you? Isn't he in prison?"

Nicolette nodded in the gloom. "Yes, in prison. Yet the Count would never confine his only son in the lower dungeons of the Castle. Surely he will be imprisoned in one of the upper chambers above the moat where air and light will reach him. We will find him. Come, we go to the dungeons."

Once more they took to the shadowed street. Noiseless as phantoms they crept down side lanes to the rear of the Castle. There across the stagnant waters of the moat the dripping dungeons loomed in black despair.

IV

The Dungeons

"MIDNIGHT and all's well."

The night watchman of Beaucaire was making his rounds. Armed with a cross bow and swinging a lantern in which a guttering candle flickered, he trudged along the street from the Castle. Betty and Nicolette shrank back into the shadows at his approach, but his keen eyes ferreted them out in the gloom.

"Ho! Who goes here?" he cried, raising his bow.

Nicolette drew her cloak closer about her face. "We go for a doctor of medicine," she answered, "my little sister and I."

"What! Two lone maids out at this hour of the night? Midnight mass has already been said by the priests in the chapel. Only the owls are out. And yet you—— By Our Lady of Lourdes, 'tis unheard of!"

The watchman blinked unbelievingly in the mellow light; his leathery face puckered with concern.

"The doctor of medicine," began Nicolette again. "My parent is ill——"

"Ill! Were I on my sick bed with a broken leg, yet would I rise before my daughter tramped the streets at this unearthly hour. Never in my years of watching—— Yes, you shall go to the bailiff's house to explain."

"Oh, but it might then be too late! My parent——"

"First then we shall go to the doctor, and I with you."

"There is no need, good watchman."

"No need! Truly, I thought something was wrong. Why do you hide your face? I have seen you before . . . 'Tis the fair Nicolette, the daughter——"

"It is true," cried Nicolette. "Yet always have you been friendly, my captain. Will you not allow me this once to go unmolested? I mean no harm."

The watchman stood thoughtful for a moment. "Never shall I forget your kindness to the people when the plague ravaged the town. . . . Yes, you may go. Nothing have I seen this night but a passing shadow. Old am I getting; my ears, when I wish, are deaf, and my mouth is tongueless. Go! I thought I heard the guardsman calling from the Market Place. Some prisoner perhaps has escaped."

He went his way swinging his lantern. His cry

echoed in the still street: "The moon's up and all's well."

Betty clung to Nicolette as they watched him disappear round a corner.

"Come, perhaps we shall find Aucassin's prison."

The end of the street was flanked by the Castle wall and the moat. No guard appeared upon the battlement; no light shone from iron-barred windows. In the serene light of the full moon the Castle was tranquilly slumbering. So still was it that Betty wondered if the river mist, rising like a magic vapor beyond the walls, had not drugged with sleep this great pile of stone above them.

Nicolette paused at the edge of the moat. "There is little water here now," she explained; "only in times of war does the Count order the moat filled."

The incessant shrilling of frogs rose from the pools. As the two made their way down the steep bank and across the damp grass the little creatures hopped away to one side or plunged with a splash into the water. Before them rose a steep bank and beyond that, sheer and unscalable, the Castle wall mounted to the luminous sky.

"See that tiny window above the bank?" whispered Nicolette. "That is the upper chamber of the dungeons. 'Tis the only one into which light and air penetrates. Surely Aucassin is there."

They glanced searchingly about them, then toiled up the slope. At the small iron-barred window they listened. The even tread of nervous feet came to them as if some wild beast were caged within.

"Aucassin, is it you?" Nicolette whispered eagerly.

The footsteps paused. "Who speaks without?" The voice was a mere croak, harsh and quavering.

Nicolette clasped Betty's hand in disappointment. "A stranger! Oh, 'tis bitter."

"Whom do you seek?" came the croaking voice.

Nicolette grasped the bars. "I seek my lord Aucassin who was thrown into the dungeons."

"Ah, well, I knew it could not be me. A youth was it? Truly, I heard the jailor clanking down the steps with a prisoner. Last evening, say you? It might have been years ago, so long seems this night. Now he lies in the chamber directly under me. For hours I have heard his weary moans."

In despair Nicolette turned to Betty. "The chamber below! But there is no window!" She was near to tears.

Betty's gaze roved along the moat. A dark

square in the bank caught her eye. "What is it? A doorway?"

Nicolette followed her to the bed of the moat. "Many times have I seen that," she answered with a shudder; "it is the iron door of the water passage. When the Count wishes to silence some prisoner in the lower dungeons, he orders it to be opened. Then the black waters pour down the passage upon the unhappy man. Oh, it is horrible!"

Betty examined the small iron barrier. "No water could enter there now, Nicolette."

"No, of course not with the moat empty."

"Do you think a voice might?"

"Oh, stupid me!" Nicolette was down on her knees, dragging at the heavy iron bolts. "Truly have you helped me this night, little gypsy. Look —it moves!"

Together they pulled the door back on its creaking hinges. A barred opening lay before them. The musty odor of stagnant air and moldy walls smote their nostrils. Eagerly they listened.

A voice sounded along the passage far below as if a spirit lay entombed beneath the earth. "Who swings back the door to drown me like a field mouse in his hole?"

"Aucassin!" Nicolette whispered. "Can you hear me? It is I——"

"Who is there?" again came the distant voice.

"Let the moat flow down into these dungeons! With my Nicolette gone I would welcome it."

Footsteps sounded from the street. Betty glanced up in dismay.

"The guard!" she warned. "They come toward the Castle."

Again came Aucassin's voice from the hollow depths: "Speak! Speak—or let the bitter waters come!"

Nicolette leaned close to the bars. "Hush, my Aucassin! 'Tis Nicolette."

"Nicolette!" There was wonder and disbelief in his tone.

"Yes, but be silent. The guard approaches."

Betty crouched behind the waving branches of a clump of willows. The steady tread of approaching footsteps drew nearer; a little group of searchers crossed to the moat. Two flaring torches threw the faces of the men into bronzed relief. She could catch their very words, so still and soft was the night about them.

"They have escaped us, I fear," said one of the searchers. "Yet are they still in the town, for the gates are closed."

"Perhaps we should search the moat, Captain."

"Yes, but here comes the watchman. He may bring us tidings."

Betty peered from between tufts of grass. The watchman with swaying lantern had joined the guardsmen.

"Have you seen aught to-night, watchman? Any travelers out?"

"Nothing, Captain."

"Then search the moat!"

The guards turned away to do his bidding. Betty's heart jumped in terror. She and Nicolette would be found and imprisoned. What could they do?

As her eyes gazed round in dismay she saw the watchman detain the men. "Captain," he interrupted, "you do not seek two helpless maids, surely."

The men wheeled at his words.

"We do! Did you see them? Where? Where?"

"I am not certain, Captain, but I thought I saw two shadows flit like ghosts from doorway to doorway ahead of me. I caught them not. They disappeared in a mist, and I thought perhaps I had stopped too long at the tavern."

"Fool!" hissed the Captain. "It may have been they. Which way went these shadows?"

"Toward the North Gate."

"The North Gate! Come, my men, we must cross the town."

The watchman quietly waited while the guards

went along the street and disappeared round a corner. Then he took up his rounds, and his cry, rocking with mirth, sounded again:

"Midnight is past and all's well!"

Betty turned with a smile toward Nicolette, but that maid was now at the passageway speaking in low tones. Betty quietly waited. The frogs about her once more began their interrupted chant. Across the sweep of the moat the shadow of the reeds grew longer; a rose-tinted gray, spreading over the eastern sky, dimmed the stars.

Presently Nicolette closed the door and joined her. "Dawn is near," she whispered; "we must make haste."

"You told him good-bye?" asked Betty softly.

Nicolette sighed. "Yes, I told him he must never see me again—but I would hide in the woods near the Abbaye of Roche de Frêne."

Quietly they crossed the moat and gained the street. An owl hooted from the Castle tower.

"The postern gate is near," Nicolette murmured.

Along the shadowed wall they crept, following the moat till it struck the town wall. "Here is the postern, little gypsy."

Nicolette reached up in the darkness and unbolted the door. As it swung toward them the hinges shrilled as if in protest against this early awakening. A faint odor of fresh wet earth came from the fields.

Before them stretched the open country, and across the vineyards the gypsy fires glowed in the dawn.

Roche de Frêne

BETTY sat on the steps of the green van. It was mid morning and the drowsy hum of insects was in the air. The camp was deserted, for the gypsies were hawking their wares about the town. Joe had taken Toto to the Market Place; Stanko had gone to the tanners to buy strips of leather for Zulieka's harness.

Betty was listening, her eyes fixed on the Beaucaire road. Would Aucassin never come! She had waited three days.

A twig snapped behind her. Nicolette touched her shoulder. "Still we wait," she said with a drooping smile.

"Perhaps he is still in prison."

Nicolette shook her head. "Yesterday the shepherds told me his father had freed him. He should have come at once."

"But if he couldn't, Nicolette?"

"Then he should have come anyway."

Betty raised her hand in warning. "Listen!"

Above the shrill of the locusts in the trees she heard the unmistakable hoof beats of a galloping horse.

"Yes, someone comes on the pathway," cried Nicolette. "Is it Stanko, think you?"

"No, that is not one of our ponies. Hide, Nicolette—in the van!"

Betty closed the door upon her, then took her seat again upon the steps.

"If it is Aucassin," came a whisper from the window, "tell him he is too late, that I have entered the holy convent of Roche de Frêne."

Between the thick foliage of the trees a white charger hove into view.

"It is he," Betty returned in a low voice. "Be quiet."

The charger reared upon its hind legs at sight of the van. Aucassin, anxious and careworn, smiled wanly when he recognized Betty.

"Oh, it is you, little friend of the gypsies. Have you seen aught of Nicolette?"

Betty solemnly nodded. "Three days ago."

"Three days ago! Where is she now?"

Betty repressed a smile. "She waited till she thought you did not care to seek her."

"Not care!" He clenched his fists till the knuckles showed white. "The day after Nicolette disappeared my father opened the dungeons to me, yet did he keep me ever under watchful eye. This morning I succeeded in stealing away. When I find my Nicolette we shall journey into a Far Country where Beaucaire cannot meddle. Tell me it is not too late!"

"I am not sure . . . She lived in a bower of green built against the walls of Roche de Frêne. You can see it through the trees."

Aucassin spurred his horse along the pathway. Betty made him out vainly searching the deserted bower.

"He suffers," Nicolette laughed from behind her. "Let him think me gone."

"You are cruel," Betty reproached her.

Nicolette wavered. "I shall let him start homeward, then call him back. Keep him near, little friend; do not let him leave."

Betty hurried along the path toward the convent wall. She found Aucassin in despair.

"Look, she has left," he cried, pointing to the empty bower. "But only recently. See, the poppies are fresh, and the wild mint is damp with dew." He paused as his eyes roved the woods about them. "Yet shall I search and find her if it takes all my days."

With rising sympathy Betty saw how tenderly he regarded the green abode. "Let me tell your fortune, Aucassin," she said. "Meg the Fortune Teller has taught me how, and I may be able to help you."

He stretched forth his hand. "If it is good news, speak; if it is bad—speak also."

She bent over his palm; tense and anxious he waited. "A long and happy life I see for you," she began in the chanting tones she had heard Meg use. She bowed her head farther to hide her smiling lips. "I see you married soon—very soon. Indeed it may be this very day!"

"This very day? If this be true I shall burn candles at the shrine of Our Lady in Egypt."

"Your search is ended before it is begun. I see a small green house on wheels. . . . Strange! Where could it be? It hides your jesting Nicolette."

He threw back his head and laughed gayly. "My brain works slowly when I think of Nicolette. A thousand blessings, little gypsy."

Betty led the way back to the green van. Aucassin followed afoot; his horse cropped the grass along the path.

"Yes, I shall return to Beaucaire," said Aucassin loudly as they neared the van. " 'Tis well perhaps that she entered the holy convent. She was ever devout and sad-eyed."

Betty heard a gasp of dismay from within the van. She glanced knowingly at Aucassin. Would Nicolette open the door? Together they waited.

"Good-bye, little friend," said Aucassin. "Now I go."

He did not turn to his horse. Instead, he suddenly sprang at a bound up the steps and flung back the door.

"What—weeping?" he asked.

"For a moment," sobbed Nicolette as she dabbed her cheeks. "I thought you cared not and were leaving me. Now I weep no longer."

"We go to a Far Country, my Nicolette. And we start at once."

Betty helped them make ready. She filled a saddlebag with food; she placed a gypsy shawl about Nicolette's shoulders. The horse pawed the ground as if eager to be off to this land beyond the hills.

Aucassin mounted his charger; tenderly he lifted Nicolette up before him. "We never shall forget you, little gypsy friend," he said; "for we owe our happiness to you."

Betty watched them ride down the leafy way toward the Abbaye of Roche de Frêne. She stood in the path waving, while softly through the thickly wooded hills came the tinkle of convent bells. A faint breeze stirred the trees at the road-side. Silent, motionless, she waited—till the swaying branches hid Aucassin and Nicolette from sight.

*Surely one of the greatest joys of
travel is the joy of returning home . . .*

STANKO

I

Good-bye to the Gypsies O!

BENEATH the late afternoon sun the gypsy caravan crept along the Great North Road. The green van led the way over gently swelling hills where sheep grazed amid wild flowers. Meadowlarks sang from the hedges, and now and then a startled rabbit bounded away into a thicket.

Stanko drowsily flicked the reins. "Did I not tell you, little ones, that we Romanys meet everyone; that around each turn of the road lies adventure?"

Betty and Joe silently nodded.

"'Twas here we picked you up one spring day," Stanko continued. "Do you remember? ... Just such a day as this."

Joe gazed across the meadow. "We were lost that day on the road, Stanko, and you said: 'We be Romany folk, too; jump up; you can have a lift and welcome to it.'"

"What wonderful adventures we've had!" Betty exclaimed. "What wonderful things we'll have to tell when we get home."

Joe gave a start. "Home!"

"Of course we must go home," Betty emphatically went on. "We've been away a long time. . . . But we don't want to leave you, Stanko."

The gypsy dropped the reins. "'Tis not for long, I hope. And neither will it be the end of adventure. As long as you keep the wonder and joy of life, always will you find adventure awaiting you around each turn of the road."

He smiled. "Whoa, Mimo! Whoa, Zulieka! Here must we say good-bye, little ones. The Romanys turn into a side lane; you go straight ahead."

Betty jumped to the ground. With quivering lips Joe followed. He patted Mimo's flanks, then rubbed the pony's nose. "Good-bye, Mimo," he whispered. "Good-bye, Zulieka!"

The little horses whinnied softly and rubbed their muzzles against his shoulders.

Betty turned to Stanko. "Won't we see you again?" she faltered.

The old gypsy nodded slyly. "Watch the road for the Romanys! Every spring we come this way. Watch the road!"

"Then we'll be here, Stanko!" Joe cried.

He drew Betty aside as Stanko turned the ponies into the lane. They heard him repeating: "On, Mimo! On, Zulieka! I drive alone to-night."

Slowly the caravan passed. Boris called out from his horse: "Next year, little friends of the Romanys! Next year!"

Meg the Fortune Teller waved good-bye. "I see you safely home," she droned. "I see——"

Breathlessly they watched the gypsies pass. What happy people! What gay caravans with their red and green paint, and their crisp white window curtains blowing in the breeze! With a tinkle of bells the caravan turned into the lane which wound toward the long blue sweep of hills. Following last went a lone horse whose small heels pattered gayly on the roadway.

Betty stood on tiptoe. "They're going over the hill," she cried. "Look, Joe, the green van is out of sight."

Joe gazed the other way. "We'd better be starting for home," he remarked. "Come on, Betty."

Once again they took to the road afoot. A steep hill faced them, and up this they quietly trudged. From a near-by hedge a bird twittered. On they went without a word between them.

Presently they came to the top of the hill. As they started down they saw below them a blue haze hanging over the countryside. The sun's rays glinted on the mist in a thousand points of light.

"It's a fog," Betty whispered. "That old fog——"

They walked on through a dream country; about them lay enchantment. Trees, hedges, shrubs, all merged into a wall of blue-gray mist. The fog clung to them with caressing dampness. Hand in hand they trailed on through the misty gloom. A weird silence brooded over the countryside; even their footfalls on the leaves of the road were noiseless.

"Let's hurry," Joe urged. "I'm sure just ahead——"

Betty quickened her steps. "It's getting lighter, Joe."

"Yes, the fog's lifting."

At the top of the second hill they paused. Somewhere in the depths of a near-by wood a bird suddenly caroled a little magic song. Eagerly the two gazed down the hillside.

"Look!" cried Betty. "There's Four Corners —and there's the Taxi Man!"

II

The Taxi Man

HE WAS standing by his taxi near a yellow road sign. When he saw them he waved his hand. "I've just repaired the tire," he called. "It was a bigger job than I thought."

Betty smiled as she came up to him. "Another tire?" she asked. "Are you always blowing out tires?"

The Taxi Man looked at her. "It's the same tire," he answered.

"Oh," said Joe, "it's another blowout, then."

The Taxi Man looked at him. "It's the same blowout," he indignantly replied.

Joe kicked one heel in the dust. "It took you a long time," he began.

The Taxi Man grinned. "I'll admit I'm not very swift. It took me all afternoon. But now I can take you two young gypsies home. Jump in."

As he threw open the door he remarked: "I thought your friends were going to bring you back."

"Oh, no," said Betty, as she stepped into the taxi; "we left the gypsies at the last turn."

"Gypsies!" cried the Taxi Man. "Did you meet some gypsies?"

"We met the Stanko tribe," Joe answered.

"You had a good time then?" inquired the Taxi Man.

"Oh, a wonderful time," Betty murmured.

"And you saw Robin Hood?"

Joe nodded. "And Charlemagne, too."

"And Nicolette—and Richard the Lion-Hearted," Betty continued.

The Taxi Man sprang to his seat. "It must have been a marvelous masquerade."

"Masquerade!" Betty gasped.

The Taxi Man turned round in his seat. His eyes were dark and somber. "Didn't you go to a masquerade party?" he slowly asked.

Joe sighed. Why did the man look so surprised, anyway? It was really quite simple. First the Taxi Man, then Stanko and his happy tribe, and now the Taxi Man again. Joe heaved another profound sigh. No, there was no use in trying to explain. Some grown-ups never would understand.

He grasped Betty's arm. "Of course we did. It seemed almost real."

"Did you find a donkey to ride?" pursued the Taxi Man.

Betty shook her head. "No, we went in a gypsy caravan."

For a moment the Taxi Man stared. Then he turned to the wheel, and as the engine throbbed threw over his shoulder:

"I'd better get you two home. We'll be there in exactly eight minutes."